Diamond: A Girl's Best Friend

6/13/09

To Debbie
"My girl"
Enjoy

Diamond: A Girl's Best Friend

A Novel

Brenda Savoy

iUniverse, Inc.
New York Lincoln Shanghai

Diamond: A Girl's Best Friend

iUniverse books may be ordered through booksellers or by contacting:

iUniverse
2021 Pine Lake Road, Suite 100
Lincoln, NE 68512
www.iuniverse.com
1-800-Authors (1-800-288-4677)

Because of the dynamic nature of the Internet, any Web addresses or links contained in this book may have changed since publication and may no longer be valid.

This is a work of fiction. All of the characters, names, incidents, organizations, and dialogue in this novel are either the products of the author's imagination or are used fictitiously.

ISBN: 978-0-595-47030-3 (pbk)
ISBN: 978-0-595-70761-4 (cloth)
ISBN: 978-0-595-91314-5 (ebk)

Printed in the United States of America

This book is dedicated to the memory of

Corey Charles Brogden

April 10th, 1971-February 21st, 2004

Acknowledgements

Although, many people from diverse walks of life gave me the inspiration to create this novel, there are five that I would like to personally thank for going the extra mile:

Angelo Robinson, PhD
Cheryl Hatcher
Rosa Hatcher Foster
Kathryn Millings
and
Joseph Giles Sermons

"But the chief problem in any community cursed with crime is not the punishment of the criminals, but preventing the young from being trained to crime."

W.E.B. Du Bois

1

the Golden Life

On a scale of one to ten, ten being the best, my life was a 9.9. I guess you could say that I had it all but the funny thing about it, is that I never realized or even appreciated it until it was gone. It happened suddenly: almost as if someone decided to pull the rug from under my feet. The rug had been my magic carpet and now I was left to topple from Utopia, into a world where I'd have to find my place, and begin all over again.

Yesterday was the 4th of July and my parents had given the biggest celebration in town. My mother went to great lengths to make sure that this party would be remembered for a long time. She'd invited all of the so-called right people to help my dad secure his seat in the state senate. Although, this would be his second win they were not taking any chances and for that reason there were celebrities, politicians and lots of who's who in attendance. As inconsequential as this festive day seemed, in time I would come to rely on its beautiful remembrances for strength to endure the tragic days ahead.

Carmen and Miles, my wonderful parents, met in their freshman year of college at Berkeley. Miles was from Baltimore and Carmen from New Orleans. After graduation they married, making California their home, settling in the small community of Carlsbad between Los Angeles and San Diego.

My dad was the youngest partner at his law firm and my mom a successful home and office interior designer. Miles was tall and muscular with black wavy hair. He was extremely handsome, very personable and always on a mission to improve the plight of the poor. My mom was very pretty and quite the conversationalist. She had a face like Halle Berry and a body like Beyonce'. I hated the stares that she got from guys whenever she visited my school. It felt as if they were disrespecting her.

They had one child, me!

My SAT scores were off the hook and major colleges were inviting me to their open houses. My parents were thrilled that I would probably get a full scholarship to the college of my choice. My mother said I should attend either Spellman or Radcliff. She felt I would devote more time to my studies if I attended a women's university but I was thinking of Howard or American University. I wanted to major in communications and work in the media. I also figured that the nation's capital would be an exciting place to study but for the moment no one was pressuring me to do anything but get good grades.

July 5th was one of those sweltering summer afternoons. Fresh cut grass, the scent of the yellow rose garden, mixed with the aroma of last night's grilled hot dogs and barbequed chicken, permeated my olfactory senses. As far back as I could remember these were the sweet smells of summer!

As I walked toward the pool, the heat from the sun caused the metal clamps attached to the sides of my thong, to burn my skin. Climbing the steps of the diving board, I could hear a familiar song from the radio of the car that just pulled into the driveway. It was Luther Vandross and Busta Rhymes singing 'A Lovely Day'. Ironically the song and memory of this last 'lovely day' would be indelibly etched in my mind.

I climbed up the diving board and did a somersault into the pool. The water was warm like a hot tub. There is something mystical about being underwater: the weightlessness and seemingly ability to exist in a dreamlike state, made me wish that I were a mermaid.

My tranquility was interrupted by the animated voice of my best friend Kennedy who'd just parked her candy apple red Mercedes in my driveway. This girl was drop-dead gorgeous but with the lowest self-esteem that you could imagine. She didn't have a clue as to how much she had going on. Poor thing spent most of her time trying to make people like her. She was so desperate to be popular that she would accept any kind of abuse or disrespect just to fit in. On one occasion while her parents vacationed in Palm Springs, she invited everyone to a party at her house. She even invited guys that had previously bashed her reputation by mixing lies, and the truth. When the party was over, no one from the in-crowd stayed to help her clean up and it actually took us three days to get her house back in order. And I will never forget the time that her dad allowed us to drive his new Bentley to shop on Rodeo Drive. As we cruised the strip, we ran into a few friends from school and they convinced her to drive to Tijuana. And just like that she said, "Yes".

"Hey Kennedy! Damn baby, you are looking good". It was Marcus, one of the guys on the basketball team at school who'd made her cry when he called her a 'ho' in front the entire football team.

He flashed his killer smile and said, "Girl we need to put that car on the road and shine."

Kennedy started blushing like he'd given her a compliment rather than the car.

She tossed her straight blonde hair around her shoulders and in her most seductive voice said, "Hello Marcus. What's happening?"

Focusing solely, on the car he answered, "Baby, you're what's happening."

"Marcus you're so crazy. Where do you think we should go?"

Marcus was dead on, in his attempt to get behind the wheel of her father's car saying, "Girl I don't believe you asking me that! Where have you been?"

Kennedy looked perplexed as Marcus continued to reel her in.

"Haven't you heard? Tijuana is off the hook on Fridays."

He took full advantage of her naivety and easily convinced her to drive to Tijuana.

She turned to me and said, "Let's do this!"

This was a perfect example of how she operated. Never giving a second thought as to how this guy previously humiliated her in front of the entire basketball team: she was down for whatever! Sometimes she was as needy as a two year old. But because I was her best friend, I couldn't let her go alone. I called home for my parent's permission: only to hear my father say that I couldn't go because we had plans to celebrate my mom's birthday later in the evening. Thank God I didn't go with her because I found out later, that she'd gotten so loaded from drinking Tequilas that one of the guys had to drive her father's car back to her house. And her parents still can't figure out what happened because she returned home half-dressed and the car had $20,000 in damages. No one including Kennedy had a reasonable explanation of what happened. Sometimes I wondered why she didn't post a permanent kick me sign on her back.

Kennedy was Bernie and Jo Silverstein's only daughter. They had two older sons who were successful entertainment lawyers. Having Kennedy at age forty-five was Jo's last attempt to save her marriage to her husband: Beverly Hills renowned plastic surgeon and aged pretty-boy. And it worked because Bernie gave up his mistresses and spent his spare time either golfing, or spoiling his beautiful daughter.

Unbeknown to my parents, Kennedy was pregnant two months ago and had an abortion because her parents thought it would be a tragedy for her to have a baby at age seventeen. Bernie and Jo adored their daughter and the very thought of her conceiving a child at such a young age was out of the question!

Michael, the boy who impregnated her denied that it was his baby and he spread a lot of nasty rumors about her. This clown was a Petey Pablo wanna be: always fronting about 'positions'. It was his claim that he had no real interest in Kennedy and that he was just out for a good time. According to him, it was one of those 'the condom broke' deals, but Kennedy insisted that they had a real relationship. In fact she swore that it was straight-up unprotected sex.

What rotten luck! Her first time and she got pregnant! Thank God her HIV test results were negative so far.

Kennedy told me that I was lucky to still have my virginity. She said, "Once the word is out that you are willing to do it. Everyone will be asking you to go out, just to see if they can do you." There were a lot of guys around school who would say that they'd had sex with her when they really hadn't. They would lie, just to look like a player and because of her reputation she was a perfect choice to lie about.

In spite of the fact that Kennedy had a bad rep, she was still my best friend. She was a talented artist, a great musician, and someone you could trust with your deepest secrets.

I surmised that she was here to hear about my date with Carl.

"Hey girl! What's sup with you and Carl? I saw you guys leave the party last night. And you didn't call me when you got in. You got something to tell me?"

Amidst all of the giggles and drama I tried to describe the passion that Carl and I shared last night. I wondered if anyone had ever made Kennedy feel that special.

"He was wonderful."

"How wonderful was he? Did he hit it?"

"Of course not!"

I saw the disappointment in her eyes as she said "Damn girl, you are probably the only girl at school who is still holding on to her V."

At that moment her expression revealed a certain pang of jealousy, as she struggled to finish her profound statement.

"Or whatever you think you're holding on to."

"That's not true because some of the girls on the basketball team and in student government are virgins."

"Yea, and look at those dweebs and nerds. Nobody knows them and nobody wants to know them! They can't even give it away. It's like they're socially non-existent. Honestly, I can't understand why you bother to talk to them."

"I talk to them because they're interesting and they're smart. Anyway virginity has its perks."

"Like what."

I couldn't think of anything to say. It was hard to match wits with someone who had so much experience in the sex arena. "Well at least guys have to respect you."

Kennedy laughed, "You need to recognize that virginity is over-rated!"

I must admit Carl was one of the cutest and smartest boys at school. All of the girls liked him but he liked me. After last night's party, we went for a ride up to Liberty Damn where we talked for nearly an hour before Carl leaned over and gave me my first real kiss. Sure I'd kissed a boy before but not with the passion that Carl and I kissed. For the first time I felt all kinds of weird sensations running throughout my body. My guess was that Carl must have also been affected because he got out of the car twice to straighten his pants. Afterwards, I didn't sleep all night and I was still restless this morning. I knew that I wanted to marry him and kiss him 24/7.

I couldn't stop talking about Carl. He was my dream come true. Kennedy said that he would be just like all of the other boys once we slept together. In my heart, I knew that she was wrong about Carl because was different from the boys that she knew. He respected me and I knew he would never ask me to do anything detrimental to our future. The plan was for Carl and me to spend our summer vacation together. I envisioned long walks at night and late night swims but as fate would have it: my parents were going to Paris for the summer. This was going to be their second honeymoon. And tonight I would be leaving for the east coast to visit my grandmother in Washington, DC, where I knew that I would die from boredom. After all, how exciting can it be to spend your summer vacation with a senior citizen? My father promised that I would have lots of fun with his mother. And how when he was growing up everyone adored her but I had not seen my grandmother since I was eight, so I vaguely remembered her.

Diamond what a strange name for a grandmother.

The Last Ride

The ride to the airport was tense, as Miles questioned Carl about school, his future ambitions and his parents. I guess this is what dads are supposed to do but I wished I could've disappeared from embarrassment.

"Young man what do your SAT scores look like?"
"I scored an overall 1500."
"Not bad. Have you thought about a major?"
"I was thinking about a career in medicine."
"What career is that?"
"Well maybe a physician's assistant."
"Why that is nothing more than a glorified nurse. Why haven't you considered becoming a doctor?"
I quickly interjected, "Carl's' father is a doctor and he's already decided that he doesn't want to always be on call and away from his family, like his dad."
My father said, "Erica why don't you let Carl speak for himself?"
Carl said, "Its' okay Erica, my dad feels the same way."
The way that my father questioned Carl, one would have thought that we were engaged.
My mother who had been unusually quiet on the ride, suddenly gave us her words of wisdom
"Miles give them a break! They are young people trying to find their way in the world." Putting her arm around his shoulder she said, "Like us they are apt to change their minds many times before they make a final decision about their future. So why don't you give them some slack? It's not as if their about to exchange vows. They're just friends!"   they're
"Thanks mom." I leaned over and kissed her on the cheek.

When we arrived at the airport I thought Carl and I would have a few minutes alone but my dad made sure that would not happen. There wasn't even the slightest chance that Carl and I would get a chance to exchange a kiss, not with my father hovering over me like I was five years old. We did however manage to exchange a quick hug, and that was the extent of our romantic goodbye. He promised to call every day and I promised that I would be there to answer.

My mom hugged me like it was the last time that I would see her and my father told me to go easy on the charge cards. I walked through security and onto my plane with thoughts of shopping in Georgetown and Tyson's corner. I'd heard a lot about Georgetown and I couldn't wait to get there. If old lady Diamond were too old to take me shopping, perhaps I'd borrow her car or catch a cab.

I slept on the plane and in between consciousness, I thought of Carl. Carl the man: Carl the boy: with whom I thought I was in love, less than twenty-four hours ago. He now seemed rather small and weak compared to Miles. If he were a real man he would have kissed me goodbye in the presence of my parents. It was at this moment that I knew that I did not love Carl. The man that I would fall in love with would be just like my dad.

2

DC and Me

It was a bright and sunny morning in Washington, DC. Reagan International Airport looked like a military camp. I guess you couldn't expect anything less with the hype of 9-11 still in full effect. I collected my baggage and went to the area where I was told to meet Diamond.

As I scanned the reception area, I saw a tall gaunt and pasty looking man, in a black suit holding a printed sign with my name on it. I walked over to the gentleman and identified myself. "Hello my name is Erica Redfern. I'm here to meet my grandmother Diamond Redfern."

'Top of the morning to you, Miss Erica: I can see the resemblance between you and your grandmother."

I mumbled a faint "Thanks." He said he would take me to Diamond, who'd sent her regrets because she was in a very important meeting, and could not come.

Sidney Hester, the driver was an Englishman with a thick cockney accent. He was tall and thin with spiked blonde hair. His salon tan, and coffee stained teeth, gave him the appearance of a poster-boy for aging male models, rather than a chauffeur. On the way to the station he tried to engage me in frivolous conversation but I avoided it by answering his questions very curtly and starring out of the window. My mother warned me not to become friendly with strangers and he was indeed a stranger! Because he kept peering over the top of his sunglasses through the rearview mirror, he appeared to be sneaky and sleazy. I wondered why Diamond had sent someone like him to pick me up.

WBIT were the letters inscribed on the tall building where Sidney parked the limo. I wondered what the acronym stood for.

Sidney escorted me to the door where I was promptly met by one of the summer interns.

"Hello my name is Shanae Butgatch and you must be Erica Redfern?" Unlike me Shanae appeared to be very confident. She was not only pretty but also graceful and pristine sort of like the kind of daughter everyone wished for. I wondered if she was going to be my competition for Diamond's attention.

Awkwardly I replied, "Yes, I'm here to meet my grandmother."

"She's in a meeting at the moment but I will escort you to her office."

The lobby was beautifully decorated with large floral arrangements. Looking around, I noticed that on one side of the lobby there was a bank and on the other side a sushi restaurant. Between the restaurant and the bank, a very attractive blind man operated a news kiosk.

The intern escorted me to an office on the 15th floor.

The conference room where the meeting was held was enclosed in glass. All of the ladies in the meeting were smartly dressed in St John, Dolce & Gabbana, Gucci, and other designer's suits. I felt out of place in my jeans and wife-beater because everyone looked like runway models.

I looked around the room for my grandmother but I did not see her. I was angry and disappointed. "Why did I come here?" Diamond was too busy to even meet me at the airport? I felt lost and alone. Just at this moment I missed my mom more than anything and I wanted to go back home! The first chance that I got, I would call my dad and convince him, that at seventeen, I was perfectly capable of staying home alone.

When the meeting adjourned several people walked up and introduced themselves, wishing me a nice vacation in DC, but I had not yet met my grandmother. Curiosity got the best of me and I walked into the conference room. As I scanned the room in search of my grandmother a beautiful well-dressed women who appeared to be in her in forties, walked up and identified herself as Diamond. I searched her face to see the resemblance between my dad and her. Her facial features were identical to Miles and mine. Yes, this was Miles' Diamond. But how could she be a grandmother? This diva could not possibly be my grandmother. Although, I had not seen Diamond in six years, I pictured my grandmother to have silver hair, low heeled shoes and a loose fitting dress. What was wrong with this woman? Didn't she realize she was a grandmother? Why was she dressed like this? Who was she trying to fool?

My thoughts were interrupted as the middle-aged diva spoke, "You must be Erica". She extended her hand for a handshake. A handshake? I couldn't believe it, not even a hug. What kind of grandmother was this?

"Yes I'm Erica." I hoped that I sounded intelligent and professional like her. God forbid that I sound like a frightened and intimidated seventeen-year old.

The truth was that Diamond looked as if she were my mother more than my grandmother. She was what you'd call a classic beauty. I looked away trying not to show my disappointment but I was disappointed, because I had been so sure that there would be lots of home cooked meals and that my grandmother would sit with me at bedtime and share stories about the good old days. This Diamond person looked as if she'd never prepared a meal in her life, and her stories about the good old days would probably be about vacationing on the French Rivera.

Diamond was the station's owner. She was in charge and you knew it. Everyone had commented that she had a propensity for success. Her presence was intimidating but mysteriously exciting and I couldn't wait to tell Kennedy about my Diva grandmother.

She checked me out from head to toe, commenting that we would be visiting 'The Mane Event' hair salon in the morning. I don't think she liked my West Coast hair do. I thought, "Who does she think she is? I liked my ponytail just fine." Besides, it was too hot for anything else. I knew that my laid back California style did not meet with her approval. In fact, I over heard her tell her friend, that her work was cut out for her. If I were such a disappointment maybe she'd send me back to California.

"Well young lady what cuisine should we have for dinner tonight. We can either go out or we can order in."

I said, "It doesn't matter" but it did matter. I wanted pizza but I was afraid that my choice would not meet with her approval. For now I would follow her lead. I thought I would go along with the program until I could figure her out.

"If you'll give me a chance to shower and change, I'd like to eat out."

"That's an excellent choice, Erica. I was afraid that you would want pizza."

She said that we'd be staying at her place in the City for tonight, rather than driving to her house in Arlington.

It was nearly six in the evening when we arrived in Georgetown. The streets were full of people scurrying in and out of quaint shops on tree-lined streets. My grandmother's Federal townhouse off the main thoroughfare of Wisconsin Avenue, exemplified the epitome of good but conservative taste. More than a house, it was her point of view: sort of a mirage of how the world appeared to her.

I recognized the varied period furniture, the contemporary art and the renaissance masters from going to work with my mother. There was an extensive collection of French handmade furnishings and 19th century American furniture on the second floor. The first floor looked less uniformed and gave way to more a modern motif with the exception of the Danish settee. The flowers in the courtyard must have been imported because I'd never seen any so rare and exquisite. This was Diamond's home, away from home. This was the place where she entertained clients, associates, and maybe even her boyfriends. I could hardly wait to see her house in Arlington. The woman appeared impeccable in every way causing me to wonder what life must have been like for my father, with Diamond as his mother.

That night we dined at a middle-eastern restaurant in Bethesda. I wore a Marc Jacobs spaghetti-strap black dress and white Prada sandals. I pulled my hair up into a fancy upsweep style trying to look sophisticated. Diamond looked pleased with my appearance.

3

A Diamond Life

Diamond Issa Califano-Redfern was born to a Somalian diplomat while he and his wife attended a conference at the United Nations. Birth on American soil gave her American Citizenship. At first there was a lot of red tape because as the daughter of a diplomat she was considered a foreign national, but in time she was declared a citizen of the United States of America. With the exception of Miles, her only child, she was the only member of her family who had been declared a natural citizen of the United States.

Diamond enjoyed the advantages of growing up on Embassy row in the nation's capitol.

The life of a diplomat's daughter was grandiose. The parties, the prep schools, and extensive travel made her a part of Washington's privileged class. After high school graduation, her parents allowed her to travel to Europe to study design at a renowned fashion house in Italy. They also gave her strict orders that after one year she was to return to the United States for college classes.

While in Rome she found a job at a top-notch design house. Her chiseled features and understated demeanor made a big hit with the top design houses and she was immediately hired as a model. In the beginning she worked for only a few hours a day, but it wasn't long before a handsome internationally renowned 25-year-old photographer became intrigued with her delicate beauty, and all at once she had more work than she could handle. In three months time, her face would appear on the cover of two international fashion magazines, and she was making more money than she ever imagined.

Her photographer, Antoine Califano was handsome and bronze: a real roughed type and she a beautiful hothouse flower. For Antoine it was love at first sight! As for Diamond, she was in love with the idea of being in love, and this man had all of the trappings to steal a young girl's heart. He owned two sport cars, a beautiful Roman casa and a Twenty-room chateau in Paris. Everyone who encountered them could tell that they were in love. The two were married in less than two months.

Antoine, who was known throughout the United States and Europe as an international playboy, shocked his friends and relatives when he married Diamond because he'd never been serious for more than a few months about any woman. So how did she land a man who was simply unattainable? What they didn't know is that Diamond kept her promise to her family. The promise was that she would remain a virgin until she married, thus forcing Antoine's hand.

Diamond spoke with her parents often during her stay in Italy, but she could not find the courage to tell them what she'd done. She could not find a way to tell them that she'd married a man, she hardly knew. In her culture it was unheard of to marry without your parents blessing. Antoine on the other hand was unaware that Diamond kept their marriage a secret from her parents. She would often awake in the middle of the night contemplating and wondering, "What if they didn't like him?" Maybe she should return to the states alone. She could tell them that she'd decided to go to college in Europe. Would they buy into that? Maybe they would disown her when they found out? Anyhow, her time in Europe was up. She'd been there for over a year and her parents were not pleased. Her father told her emphatically to return home for fall college classes.

Antoine insisted on traveling with Diamond to the United States to meet her parents because he wanted to meet with their approval but she needed more time to figure everything out. She devised several plans but the most practical one was to have them meet Antoine at a public outing, where there would be little time for questions, or her father's wrath. Of course the introductions would be brief, with no mention of the marriage. Yes, she would be able to conceal her marriage until her parents were ready. Two days before it was time to travel to the United States, Antoine was called to do a photo shoot at the home of his friend Carmine Andolini.

Carmine, an internationally celebrated designer, was noted for his signature handbags and scarves. His home was absolutely breath taking with its Olympic size glass enclosed pool, endless rose gardens and an atrium larger than the average Roman casa, all resting upon 13 acres of unbelievable rugged landscape.

Tourists came from the world over just to get a view of this awe-inspiring eighth wonder of the world.

This morning it was very noticeable to Diamond that Antoine was doing the careful dressing thing, which was unusual for an early morning photo shoot. Normally he was unshaven and a bit unkempt for an early morning job but today he was manicured from head to toe.

As Antoine left the house, Diamond yelled teasingly, "I hope she's worth all the effort", implying that he was going to flirt with his new model. Antoine told his beautiful bride, "This won't take long, a couple of hours at the most. We can meet later for lunch." In fact he promised her that he'd probably be gone for a couple of hours but he must have been gone for most of the morning. At noon Diamond became impatient and decided she would surprise her husband and meet him for lunch. She must have dialed Carmine's home ten times before she decided to drive to meet her husband.

As she drove the countryside, the daffodils seemed to nod at her in unison, as if they were in agreement with her sentiment that today was the happiest day of her life. Without a cloud in the sky, the sun wore the biggest smiling face ever. Everything was perfect! She was going to meet her handsome husband for lunch, to be followed by an afternoon of passionate lovemaking.

Diamond pulled into the driveway of Carmine's mansion around noon and spotted Antoine's car. She knocked at the door but didn't get an answer, so she decided to walk to the back of the mansion. She met Constantine (Carmine's houseboy) as she entered the house.

Constantine was tall, very dark, with thick black hair. And even with his weather beaten skin and red eyes (obviously from too many drinks the night before), you could easily detect that he had been a real looker. Diamond said, "Hello Connie, I'm looking for Antoine."

Constantine never spoke a word but very condescendingly directed her to the pool area. Everyone always commented that Constantine was amusingly arrogant because he owned nothing but the clothes on his back but acted as if he were royalty. At eighteen he'd left Italy for Hollywood to become a movie star. After a few years of one disappointment after another, he returned to Rome and fell prey to alcohol and drugs. Carmine took him in as a favor to his family. Although, Carmine treated him like a servant, it was rumored that they were lovers.

Diamond's imagination ran wild as she envisioned the photo shoot to be with some Italian beauty, probably barely clad in a bikini. In fact Carmine and her husband were probably marveling over this beauty right now. She thought she would tease Antoine about his attraction to the model over lunch.

Nothing in her short life prepared her for what she was about to witness. As she entered the pool area she saw three nude men: two were passionately kissing in the pool while the other sat poolside smoking a joint.

This could not be happening. Antoine, her husband, the love of her life was actually kissing another man.

Was she dreaming? Her stomach was all at once in knots and she felt her heart would jet from her body. She couldn't speak. She wanted to scream, cry and curse but the words would not come.

Antoine stood straight up in the pool: his manhood suddenly flaccid from the shock of his wife's presence, "Diamond, I can explain. Please let me explain!"

What was there to explain?

Diamond felt as if she were trapped in a nightmare and momentarily she couldn't discern if she were dreaming. But this was not a dream. It was real? Yes, this was as real as the smirk on Constantine's face, as she bolted from the house. Her superfine relationship with her husband was a farce! This was absolutely the worst day of her life.

She was completely unaware that Antoine was bisexual. How could she have been so blind? Hadn't there been signs? The late nights that he swore he was playing cards with the fellows. And what about the late night photo shoots? Yes, when she thought about it there had been many signs but she was too young and naïve to make a connection. She would learn later that Antoine exchanged sexual favors for work. This was the reason he was able to rise to the top, so quickly in a business that took most people 10 or more years to peak.

Disillusioned and heart broken Diamond returned to Antoine's villa. She collected as many of her things as she could and checked into a nearby hotel. She never wanted to see Antoine again. Whatever she was feeling at this moment, she knew that she must hide it in her heart.

Two days later Diamond was on her way back to the states alone. Her marriage to Antoine Califano would forever be her secret.

A Real Love

College was an exciting time in Diamond's life. The late sixties and the early seventies was the age of the hippie. The clothes as well as the students were wild. Platform shoes, bell-bottoms, elephant leg pants, mini-skirts, Afros, long hair and marijuana were the norm of the day. Many young men enrolled in college to avoid the Vietnam War.

With everyone looking for a cause, people protested for, and against everything. Four students were killed in Diamond's first semester on her college campus. The event gained worldwide attention and inspired the Isley Brothers and Jimi Hendrix, to record the song, 'Ohio/Machine Gun".

'Free Love' and 'Love Thy Neighbor' was posted on the door of Diamond's dorm. Everyone was either in love or looking for love.

Diamond's roommate Shannon Petes was from Boston. Shannon immediately recognized Diamond from her picture on the cover of 'Trend' magazine. Shannon, the scheming opportunist learned to piggyback off Diamond's cover girl image. After all, the more she publicized that her roommate was a former cover girl, the more dates she would get. If Shannon wanted a certain guy she would tell his friend that she could set him up with Diamond, if he would hook her up with his friend. Unfortunately, Diamond had no interest in a serious relationship with anyone, and she really meant it: that is until she met Clayton Redfern.

Clayton mesmerized Diamond with his good looks and seemingly good intentions.

Diamond swore that she'd never love again but Clayton was different from the other guys on campus. It didn't matter to him that she'd traveled to Europe and became an international cover girl. He didn't fall head over heels in love with Diamond. Unlike the other guys she'd dated, he was quiet and reserved. There was nothing whirlwind about their courtship: in fact it was slow and easy. Clayton was a fifth year engineering student and the Resident Assistant for the senior dorm. He was very easy on the eyes and quite the athlete. You could look at him, and tell that he was destined to be great.

At first, getting beyond the hurt to begin a new relationship seemed impossible for Diamond because she was badly damaged. The pain from her broken marriage to Antoine left her insecure and defensive. But Clayton proved through his actions time and time again that he was truly her soul mate, and he would always be there for her.

Diamond's parents, who'd always insisted that their children marry someone of their own culture, soon changed their minds after meeting Clayton Redfern. Clayton was so cool and polished that her parents gave her their approval of him at once.

They married in her junior year and seven months later Miles was born.

After graduation, Diamond pursued a career in the media and Clayton in environmental and civil engineering. Both excelled in their careers and it was often commented by friends, that they were the ideal couple. They shared the kind of love that is so rare among married couples because after 13 years they were just as in love as the first day that they met. They had it all, and Miles was the joy of their lives.

They settled into a four-story house in the Bolton Hill community of Baltimore.

Clayton had aspirations of running for political office, and Diamond wholeheartedly supported his ambition.

It was a perfect fall day in mid-October of 1984. The temperature was 75 degrees and the mahogany sunflowers in the courtyard were in full bloom. Clayton left work early with one thing on his mind: good sex with his beautiful wife. His workday had been long and difficult. The very thought of his wife's nude body under his appeared to be the greatest reward that life had to offer.

He had not been in the house for more than five minutes when Fed X arrived with a letter from Italy, addressed to Diamond Califano. He asked the Fed X driver if he'd made a mistake because his wife's name was Diamond Redfern. After calling for verification the driver said he had the correct party. Clayton accepted the letter with the thought that 'Califano' was the name that Diamond used while working as a model in Europe.

As Diamond left her office on the fifth floor of the 'World Trade Center' she noticed that the traffic around Baltimore's 'Harbor Place' was almost at a stand still. It was unbelievable that Baltimore had become a national tourist attraction. As a child she'd heard Washingtonians often refer to Baltimore as a dirty water-front, blue-collar town. She wondered what the critics would say now, if they could see this magnificent urban renaissance with it grand hotels and restaurants.

Walking to her car she thought of how she would surprise her family by taking them to one of the seafood restaurants at the harbor for dinner tonight. She wanted nothing more than to please the men in her life and both Miles and Clayton loved seafood. While stuck in traffic she used the time to reflect on her family's upcoming vacation and the happiness of visiting her husband's home on the Arizona 'reservation' would bring to their son Miles.

The Hopi Indian reservation proved to be a wonderful and exciting place for children. Miles loved visiting the reservation and playing with his many cousins. Grandpa Redfern taught Miles how to survive on the land. At thirteen, Miles knew how to hunt wildlife and fish. The Pow-Wow was the most spectacular event, as Clayton always dressed in full regalia for the men's traditional dancing, while Miles performed in the competitive fancy and grass dancing. The women in Clayton's family taught her many Indian customs and traditional recipes. She was ecstatic and could not wait to make the long drive across country to Arizona.

As she entered the house, Clayton presented Diamond with the letter and hung around to hear about its contents.

Diamond opened the letter and suddenly she became visibly ill. The letter read Antoine Califano died over a month ago. Antoine's demise was sure. The letter read that he'd died from a disease that the world knew very little about: 'Acquired Immune Deficiency Syndrome'. The letter read that because Antoine never remarried and did not have a living will, Diamond stood to inherit more than fifteen million dollars from his estate and the chateau in Paris.

Until now her marriage to Antoine had been her secret for all these years. How would she explain it to Clayton?

Attempting to regain her composure she said, "Baby, we need to talk."

She told Clayton of her of marriage to Antoine and how she was so ashamed of it that she never told anyone. She thought he would be sympathetic but he was furious.

"Diamond, why didn't you tell me? Why did I have to find out this way?"

"I wanted to tell you many times but I was afraid."

"What were you afraid of, other than the truth?" "What else did you lie about?"

"Nothing,"

"Did you ever divorce him?"

"No. I mean not really."

"What do you mean not really? Do we have a marriage or not?"

It hadn't crossed her mind that because she and Antoine never divorced, her marriage to Clayton was bogus.

She tried hard to circumvent the issue by saying, "Clayton lets go to Italy, and resolve this matter together. Just think about how the money could help us to fulfill all of our dreams."

"Don't talk to me about dreams when we're in the middle of a nightmare. Please explain to me why I should to go to Italy? I didn't just inherit fifteen million dollars from my former wife's estate!"

Her tone was desperate as she said, "I was thinking that on the plane over to Italy, we could decide what to do with the money."

Clayton was livid "The money is yours. I don't want his money! You go to Europe and settle your husband's affairs!"

"He's not my husband! You are my husband!"

"Why don't you cut the bullshit? Technically you are no longer married to him because he's dead and legally you aren't married to me either!"

"Clayton, what are you saying?"

"Okay, let me break it down for you. Let's talk about the fact that we aren't legally married." His eyebrows were raised and his voice was exceptionally loud indicating that he was furious. In all of the thirteen years of their marriage Clayton had never raised his voice in anger at her.

"Please don't talk like that. The money is not important. We can give it all away and we can get married tonight!"

Miles hearing all of the commotion came into the room. "Hey guys, what's going on? Did mom wreck the car again?"

Clayton mumbled in a low tone, "No son, just our lives."

"Miles darling, why don't you walk the dog?"

"Why is it that every time you guys get in a big discussion, I have to walk the dog?"

"Miles don't question your mother, just do what she says."

"Okay. I'm outta here."

Diamond tried to put her arms around Clayton but he pushed her away. "Clayton you have to believe that I wanted to tell you but I was afraid."

"In all of the thirteen years that we've been together you didn't think to mention that you were married to someone before me?"

She lowered her head in shame as he raged on. "Woman my heart is aching and the truth is I don't think that I can ever trust you again!"

"You can trust me! And I want you to know that I don't give a damn about the money."

"I know how much money means to you. And you and I both know that you aren't about to give one dollar of that money away and you shouldn't. After all you earned it! Maybe you should use the money to start a new life because I don't think that I can handle this one with you."

"I swear I'll do what ever you want me to."

"Diamond, I love you more than life itself." Stumbling over each word and fighting back the tears he managed to say, "What I mean is that, I thought that if anything ever happened to you, I wouldn't want to live anymore. Now do you understand how hurt I am?"

"I'm so sorry. I never meant to hurt you. You have to believe me"

"Whether I believe you or not, doesn't matter."

"What are you saying?"

"I'm saying that I don't think that I can forgive this!"

With tears streaming down her face she pleaded, "Baby please, give another chance."

Clayton grabbed his jacket and headed out to the car."

She called out to him but he picked up his pace, started the car, and drove off in a fury.

In the days that followed, Diamond insisted that she and Clayton both test for HIV. Dr. Wallace said it was highly unlikely that Diamond had contracted HIV from Antoine because it had been more than fourteen years since her marriage to Antoine, and by now there would have been symptoms. Although, the test results were negative, Clayton was infuriated. His pride had been tested, and taken to the limit because he could not conceive of the only woman that he'd ever loved being so deceptive.

For months they tried to work it out with the help of marriage counseling but to no avail.

While Diamond and Miles went to Europe to settle Antoine's financial matters, heartbroken Clayton resigned from his job and made plans to return to the reservation alone.

When Diamond returned to the states, they came to terms resulting in an amicable separation. It was agreed that neither would tell anyone about their bogus marriage, and Miles would spend every summer on the reservation with his father.

Diamond soon came to the realization that she'd destroyed her marriage by not telling the truth. She wondered, "What would she do without this perfect man?" "How would she live?"

She vowed that after Clayton left that she would never fall in love again: and she thrust her whole being into being a successful businesswoman and mother. No man would ever get close enough to hurt her again! In the years that followed, there would be countless dates and a few significant affairs but none would have the magic that she shared with Clayton Redfern.

4

Dear Diary

Kennedy called everyday to keep me informed of the happenings on the west coast. We'd already started making plans for our senior year of high school. I planned to audition for the varsity cheerleader squad and Kennedy would play sax in the marching band. We vowed never to be seen in the same outfit twice.

I fantasized about the prom and whether or not I would run for prom queen. Would my friendship with Kennedy impact my chance to win? Who would be my date? Would Miles rent a limo for me or would my date drive? I'd already begun to design my prom dress. I wanted it to be spectacular.

I thought about my house and mostly about my room, and I wondered if Tina the housekeeper had allowed her children to play in my room without my permission. Tina was our pretty Hispanic housekeeper, who always brought her children to work on their days off from school. The 5 year old was loud and bratty while the 10 year old was really a cool kid. My mother didn't like the idea of the children coming to work with their mother but Tina talked first to my father and he'd said it was okay.

Miles commented that Tina lived in section eight housing and that it would be good for her children to see another side of life. He said, "Maybe it will give the kids the inspiration needed to succeed in life" … Sometimes it seemed that my father wanted to help the entire world. His constant philanthropy and charitable acts often annoyed Carmen, as well as me.

I was really looking forward to my senior year in high school. I was president of the debate team and vice president of student government. Mr. Rodriquez, my science teacher said I was a natural leader. If I were a leader, it was because my parents encouraged me to reach for the stars. I knew that this year was going to be the best year of my life.

A lot of my friends had already lost their virginity. Most of the guys that they'd slept with had moved on to conquer new territory, leaving them heartbroken and confused, about love and life.

I thought about Sommer Wainwright who tried to kill herself because her boyfriend dumped her. She actually tired to hang herself in her family's garage. If the rope had not broken causing her to fall and break her leg, she'd be dead. She'd fallen so deeply in love with super jock Jamal Greer that she felt her life had no purpose when he said goodbye to her, to date her best friend. His explanation for leaving her was that he wanted a nice girl. But she was a nice girl until she gave in to him.

I thought I would wait until college before getting into the sex game. It sounded so complicated, especially with the fear of catching an STD, or of possibly getting pregnant.

In our health class we learned how to use a female condom to go along with the male condom. One day during class one of the boys blurted out that he couldn't achieve an orgasm when wearing a condom. Our health teacher told him not to worry and that he should continue to masturbate as usual. The class went into hysterics.

5

'Street Life in the Nation's Capital'

I was beginning to think differently about Diamond. Not only was she outwardly beautiful but she was caring as well. I was becoming her creation and I loved it! At seventeen, I looked like an executive with my designer suits, and new shoulder length haircut.

My days at WBIT were spent in meetings with lots of important people. I guess you could say that I was learning the business and Diamond loved introducing me to everyone. It was while visiting Washington that I decided to become a talk show host. Diamond often commented to acquaintances, "I'd like you to meet the up and coming Oprah." She told me that one way to become a successful talk show host was to watch Oprah and study her style. She said "Make Oprah your role model, after all she is the best in the business." That is exactly what I did. Everyday at 4: o'clock I went to Diamond's office to check out Miss Oprah. Today was a repeat of Oprah's fiftieth birthday party. I asked Diamond if she could arrange for me to meet Oprah.

She laughed, "It would probably be easier to meet the President but I'll do my best."

On my birthday Diamond took me to dinner at Toney Brown's Restaurant in Georgetown. It was during dinner that she presented me with a four-carat diamond Tiffany's bracelet that had been passed down to her from her mother. She told me that I should only wear it on special occasions and that I should pass it on to my daughter when she became of age.

"Erica, this bracelet belonged to your great grandmother Aminah. You must be very careful when you wear it. I want you to pass it on to your daughter or

24

granddaughter. Now I want you to promise me that you will help to keep this tradition in our family." I let out a big yell of "Yes!" Diamond laughed and told me to calm down. I was so excited that I could hardly catch my breath! My very first diamond bracelet! I pulled out my cell phone and called my parents to tell them. They were having lunch at a café on the Champs Elysees in Paris. My mother told me to be careful not to lose it, and my dad said, "Congratulations, every princess should have a diamond bracelet."

When Sydney returned to pick us up after dinner, his niece Meagan was with him.
"Meagan I would like for you to meet Miss Erica Redfern."

"What's up Erica?"

I nodded my head "Hello, nice to meet you."

Sidney's niece, Meagan Shanahan was a sophomore at Georgetown University. A part-time model from England, she was at least 5 ft 10inches tall without heels and probably weighed about 110 lbs. She was flat-chest with short red hair and green eyes. I liked her style of dress: it was different from anything that I'd ever seen. I couldn't say that she was pretty but her look was very interesting, and I loved her accent.

"Say Erica, What'd you say we run about town one evening? Maybe we could hang out at Sleepers or the Sparkle?"
Before I got a chance to answer, Diamond said, "Thanks Meagan, for the invite but Erica's got a really busy schedule." I didn't like Diamond being so over protective. It was almost embarrassing.

Megan said, "Okay. Maybe I'll holler back at ya when something is happening."

Later that evening Diamond told me that Meagan was wild, and an opportunist and that I needed to stay focused on my goals. For sure I have goals, with my future perfectly outlined, but I was also a kid from California who wanted to have some fun in the nation's capital.

On the following Friday, I got a call from Meagan, asking me to hangout. After a lot of promising and begging, Diamond told me to be careful and Meagan promised to have me home by eleven thirty because my curfew was twelve midnight.

A Taste of Honey

It was a sultry and mystical night in the nation's capitol. I felt energized as we rode thru downtown Washington in Meagan's white convertible Jeep. When it came to music Meagan was old school all the way. She put Sly and the Family Stone in the CD player, pumped up the volume and we jammed to 'Hot Fun in the Summer time', as we rode around downtown checking out the guys. She sounded really awful singing "The end of the spring and then she comes back: those summer days: those summer days." So this is how college kids act. It wasn't any different from how high school kids act. For the first time in my life I felt a sense of real liberation. I was in a place where no one knew me and I could do whatever I wanted, without repercussions from my parents.

Around 10 p.m. Meagan pulled up to a club called 'Sleepers' on Constitution Avenue. This would be my first experience in a club that sold alcohol. Just as we were about to be carded at the door, Meagan reached into her purse and slipped something into the hand of the bouncer. The bouncer smiled and we got in with no questions asked. I asked, "How did you manage that?"
Meagan laughed, "Manage what?"
I said, "You know. Getting us into the club without being carded?"
She smiled, "In time, but for now don't sweat the technique."

It was evident that Meagan frequented this club because everyone knew her. I heard a couple of guys saying things like

"Man did you see the dime with Meggie?"
"Man that new diva is a bomb."
"She's a ten all the way."
It felt good that college guys thought that I was a ten. I walked through 'Sleepers' feeling like a dream girl.

And then there was Justin, a junior at Howard University. He was finer than fine and his nickname was Slick. Slick looked like a real trendsetter with class and style. What a body! What a face! He was standing in front of me and looking straight into my eyes. I could tell that I was out of my league because I didn't know what to say. I didn't want to sound like a high school senior but what could I talk to him about. I couldn't believe that a sophisticated college man was interested in me.

It was without hesitation that Meagan introduced me as her little sister. I was cinnamon brown in color and I was being introduced as the sister to the whitest white girl that I'd ever met. Imagine that! Slick never blinked when Meagan made the introduction. We talked for a few minutes and then he asked me to dance. We danced to John Legend's 'Ordinary People' and Keith Washington's old school "Kissing You". He held me in a way that made my body curve into his and it felt so good. I was beginning to feel those same sensations that I'd felt with Carl, the night before I left California.

At the end of the dance I allowed him to kiss me. His lips were soft and somewhat moist and I could taste wine on his tongue. I don't understand why I let him kiss me, but it seemed very natural, and I was more than excited. I was ecstatic!

He held my hand when he walked me back to the table. He walked and I floated. After that the conversation was smooth and easy.

He asked me, "Who do you belong to?"

Stumbling over my words I managed to say "Nobody. I mean I'm from California." I sounded just like a kid, and I wanted so desperately to sound grownup.

He smiled at me and said "Slow down young lady. Am I making you nervous? I just want to know if you've got a man and if so, is he here with you?"

For a fleeting moment I thought about Carl back in California and about the promises that we made to each other. But I made the snap decision that he wasn't really my man and I found myself answering "No I don't have a man."

"Do you think I could be your man?"

I said "I'm not sure because we just met."

I didn't know what to say because I wasn't quite sure what he meant. Did he mean that I would have to have sex with him, if he were my man? I wasn't ready for that kind of a commitment. In all actuality, I was afraid.

He laughed as if he'd read my mind. "You are just as sweet as you are pretty? I would like to take you out tomorrow night if you're not busy?"

Busy? He must be crazy! I could never be too busy to be with him.

I eagerly responded, "What time do you want to meet?"

When he asked for my cell number I gave it to him without any reservation, and agreed to meet him on Saturday night. I was thankful that he didn't ask me how old I was.

I arrived home at exactly 12:05 am, to find Diamond waiting up for me. We talked briefly about my evening but I didn't dare tell her that I had been to a real club. It was so weird because Diamond was starring at me in the strangest way, almost as if she knew what happened tonight. It was almost as if she could read my mind.

"How was your evening, Erica?"

"It was a good evening."

"So what did you do?"

"Nothing, we just rode around town for awhile."

"You rode around town for six hours?"

"No not the whole time. But we rode mostly around the City. Oh yeah, and we stopped to get something to eat."

I soon discovered that I was not a very good liar because I was having a lot of trouble making up this story. I wasn't at all like my best friend Kennedy, who could lie so convincingly to her parents, that even though they knew that she was lying, they believed her.

"Grandmother, I'm really tired. Can we talk in the morning?"

Diamond had a perplexed look on her face as she leaned over and kissed me "Good night Erica. We'll talk in the morning."

I went to bed trying to scheme on getting out tomorrow night. I didn't want to lie to Diamond but I had to see Justin again.

I called Meagan very early the next day, and told her that I really needed her help because I just had to be with Justin tonight.

"Hello Meagan, its Erica." Not giving her a chance to respond I asked "Meagan I need a big favor. Please pick me up at seven thirty and say that we are going late night shopping at the Mazza Galleria."

Meagan asked, "What are you up to?"

"Justin wants me to meet him tonight."

Meagan hesitated at first but then agreed to help me. "Erica, I don't want any trouble from Diamond or my uncle. You need to handle your business so that it doesn't fall back on me."

"Don't worry about Diamond. I'll handle my grandmother, if you promise to pick me up."

It was easy for Meagan to get away with Sidney working all the time. Diamond on the other hand was more than suspicious when I asked to go out but she eventually gave in.

We pulled up on Wisconsin Avenue outside of the Mazza Galleria around 7:30pm. Justin and Sean were waiting for us: looking at us as if we were something to be devoured.

Meagan was wearing 'Trash Couture's' creation of a pink and green feather edged dress that glided over her tall lean body: while I wore a short black-capped sleeve dress and Jimmy Cho black ankle strapped shoes.

Justin didn't have any definite plans. We just wanted to be together and so we walked around holding hands, watching people admire, and hate us.

It was while in the mall that Justin got a call. He walked away as if he didn't want us to hear his conversation and when he came back he looked upset. He said he had to make a run and he would join us later. He told Sean to take us to the 'Sparkle' and wait outside for him. I felt awful that Justin had to leave in the middle of our first date. I wondered if it was bad news from home.

Meagan said that the 'Sparkle' was a young adult nightclub that had four floors of entertainment. I couldn't wait to get there.

We arrived at the club at 9: o clock and waited outside for nearly an hour before Justin showed up. While we waited, Sean told us to check out the tens, the hoes, the shot callers and the ballers, standing in line to get in. These people went all out to dress and impress. The smells of 'arizona and purple haze' were in the air.

Justin drove up around ten. He jumped from his SUV and announced that he was taking us to dinner rather than going into the club and he wanted us to ride in his new Hummer. It was brand new, black and shiny with spinners. Wow!

I didn't know where we were having dinner but I wanted to freshen up. I asked Meagan to go inside to the ladies room with me. We could not have been gone for more than five or ten minutes. When we returned police were all over the place and Justin and Sean were in handcuffs. I had heard these things happened in the inner city but I had never witnessed it before. Was he being arrested for driving while black? If so, this was discrimination! Or maybe the cops thought the car was stolen? I was determined to find out! I made my way through the crowd, walked up to one of the officers and asked what happened "Why are they in handcuffs?" The officer asked, "Do you know these drug-dealers?" At that moment Meagan grabbed me by my arm and told me to shut-up and come with her. I was in a state of shock. Was Justin a drug-dealer? This man, with movie star qualities couldn't possibly be a drug dealer.

What I didn't know is that Justin Black was dropped from Howard University's role for poor scholarship more than a year ago, but he still continued to hang around the campus crowd. He was a well-known drug dealer on and off campus. Justin Black was a Bama from Alabama who got caught up in the drug scene, trying to keep up with the playas'. I would later find out that he was facing 10 to 25 years on conspiracy and possession with intent to distribute charges.

6

'The culture clash'

Justin Black

Justin was from a family of migrant workers in Alabama. Getting a scholarship to college made him the top dog in his family. When his parents spoke of him it was with great pride because he graduated valedictorian of his high school class, and he was the first in his family to attend college. It was noted in his high school yearbook that he was 'Most likely to Succeed'.

Justin had long ago made up his mind that he would not be a part of a plantation system: a system that was what he considered to be a step above slavery. What else was share cropping but an extension of slavery? He hated the fact that his family rented land and housing from a white racist family. Finding employment off campus, he vowed never to return home: not even on semester break. He was going to be the one to break the cycle!

After his high school graduation Justin enrolled at the Mecca of Black Colleges, Howard University. When he arrived on campus he was quickly labeled a Bama because he lacked style. In his first semester he met Skip Crenshaw a junior from San Francisco. Skip had a GQ look: sort of like he just stepped of the cover. The first day that Justin met Skip, Skip was wearing a Gucci leather jacket, a Brioni silk shirt, and shearling boots. Justin by contrast was wearing a played out brown bomber jacket, a pair of faded jeans, and off-brand tennis. The two met while standing in line to purchase books, and they bonded from the very beginning.

Skip said, "Hey nephew, where you from?"

Justin trying to be friendly answered, "I'm from Alabama."

"You know for some reason I could tell."

"How's that?"

"Well to be honest with you. You got a Wal-Mart look going on."

"Excuse me."

Laughing, Skip said, "No, excuse your country ass."

At that point Justin stepped up to Skip, looked him straight in the eye and said, "Do you want to repeat what you just said."

"Damn man! Don't get serious on me. I was just messing with you. Let me buy you breakfast and show you around campus. I would like to turn you on to some of the fine women on campus."

Justin suspiciously asked, "Why would you do that for me?"

"Lets just say that you remind me of myself, when I first got here."

At that point Justin felt at ease.

As time went by his attraction to Skip was much more than the way he dressed: it was how he handled women. Justin was in awe of how Skip dated girl-friends and the girls didn't seem to mind. They just wanted to be in Skip's company.

His words of wisdom to Justin were, "Every woman is a bitch, and like a female dog, the worst you treat them, the more they love you. On the other hand you got to be careful of 'ho's' because' ho's' don't love nobody, not even themselves."

Skip liked Justin because he seemed smart as if he could handle himself in difficult situations. Skip on the other hand was looking to expand his drug market 'by any means necessary', while Justin's aim was to get rich quick. Skip easily lured the gullible country boy in just by asking him if he was satisfied with his financial situation. When Justin responded no, Skip seized the opportunity to bait him in.

Justin had been referred to as a raga-muffin by the upper-classmen on campus, and he was ready to do any thing to change his image. Skip told him how he could look good, and have the women falling at his feet. He also explained how easy it was to make big money fast.

Six months later Justin was wearing designer hook-ups and he'd become well versed in street lingo. One year later, the shy Southern Baptist Christian young man, had become a well-known dealer on and off campus in DC.

Pretty boy Sean, Justin's sidekick, was just that. Sean wasn't a user or a dealer but a pre-med student who liked hanging around with flash and bling-bling, and unless a miracle happened, he was facing time mainly for guilt by association.

Meagan and I caught a cab back to her car. On the way home she told me some cruel truths about life that I was not prepared to deal with. She started out by telling me that black guys with expensive cars and clothes like Justin's were usually into something illegal.

I told her that where I come from all of the guys have nice clothes and cars and their parents bought them.

She said, "Da! Hey valley girl! You're no longer in Tinsel Town! Welcome to the real world!"

What was real about assuming that every black guy who was well dressed with a nice car was a drug-dealer? To make things worse she said, that before she met Diamond, she thought all black people were poverty-stricken or drug dealers. I asked her if she really felt this way why did she make it a point to only date black men. She laughed, "Once you go Black, you never go back!" I wasn't exactly sure of what that meant but I knew I didn't want to hangout with her again.

The next day I felt as if I were in the middle of a nightmare. I'd decided to sleep in because I needed time to digest what really happened last night. I told Diamond that I didn't feel well.

My cell phone rang off the hook all morning. When I finally answered, it was Justin Black asking me to do him a favor. He wanted me to take some money to Elite Bail Bond and post bond for him. Now as I look back over everything that happened, he never gave me the chance to express how I felt.

"Hey Erica, I'm sorry about last night. Please don't be angry with me."

"I am not angry, just disappointed. And I don't understand."

"Listen up Baby Girl, as soon as I get out I will make it up to you and put you down with everything. But right now I need you to do me a big favor. You know that my peeps live out of town and I really can't trust anyone but you. What I'm saying is that I need you to handle my business for me but you gotta say that you trust me."

He talked so fast that I got lost in his words. I heard the words coming from my mouth, "Yes Justin, I trust you."

"Listen to me baby girl. Do I look like a drug-dealer? You know how the cops like to set us up. They got a thing for trying to bring a young brother down."

Because I'd heard my Dad, as a defense attorney, say the exact same thing on many occasions, regarding his clients, it was easy to buy into what Justin was saying.

"Erica I need to know if you believe me? And if you believe me, will you help me?"

Justin's voice was warm, seductive, and charming, and I said yes before I realized what I'd been asked to do.

"Yes Justin I believe you and I'll do whatever you want me to do."

I showered, bumped my hair, and dressed so perfectly that I caught the eye of everyone that I encountered. My mother taught me that your outer appearance was your calling card and the rest depended upon what you had inside.

The address I was given was for an apartment above a bar on Hanover Place and North Capital in the northwest area of the city. The stench of stale cigarette smoke and urine greeted me as I climbed the stairs to Moe's third floor apartment. Two little girls with the dirtiest faces I'd ever seen played a game of jacks on the stairs. The younger girl tugged at my purse as I walked by. The girls looked neglected and I wanted to give them a few dollars to get something to eat but I thought it might involve me in something else that I didn't want to be a part of.

I knocked on the door, and was greeted by a middle-age man who was naked from the waist up. His bloated stomach hug over his pants and his breath smelled of cigarettes and whiskey. I told him that I was there to pick-up a package for Justin.

"Hello, I'm Erica. Justin sent me here to pick up some money for his bond."

The man stood back in amazement and stared, asking "Girl, you sure you ain't 5-0?"

"No sir, I am a friend of Justin's."

"Come on in Baby Girl", he said looking out over my shoulder and down the hall. "You know I got to be sure because you can't trust any body these days."

I walked into the moldy smelling apartment with my nose in the air. Moe told me to have a seat but I said no thanks. I couldn't imagine sitting on this sofa that probably would have left a stain on my clothes.

There were faded blue curtains at the front windows, a frayed blue carpet on the floor and a deck of cards on a badly scratched coffee table.

"No thanks, I'll stand."

"Okay baby girl. Just give old Moe a minute to get things together", and he disappeared into the next room.

For the minute or two that I was alone in the room, my mind wandered back to my parents and to Diamond. What would they say if they saw me in a place like this? How did I become involved in Justin's nightmare? I didn't sell or use drugs. Why was I here? Why couldn't Moe post bond for Justin?

Moe returned with two packages. He said that he needed me to drop a package off for him before going to post bond for Justin. I told him that I didn't know my way around town and that I was visiting from L.A.

Moe looked at me from head to toe and said, "Damn girl, I need to move to Los Angeles."

I almost laughed when he said it because I could imagine anything but Moe in my neighborhood.

The real truth is that I didn't trust this Moe person. I felt anxious and I wanted out of this. I wanted to run to my car, and take off like the speed of lightning, but a promise is a promise and maybe this was all a big mistake. What if Justin was legit? It was inconceivable that anyone as fine as Justin could possibly be bad and I wanted so desperately to believe in him.

"Baby Girl, I am only asking you to do this favor because you're Justin's girl, and I know I can trust you, and you know you can trust me. Justin told me that you would be willing to do me the favor." Suddenly, his demeanor changed. He looked serious as he asked, "We don't have a problem, do we?" I was frightened but I didn't want to show it

"No just tell me where to go."

I just wanted this to be over as quickly as possible.

In a matter of hours I was doling out my trust to two individuals who had not earned it.

Moe stood very close to me as he gave me written directions to the drop-off point. He took this opportunity to run his hand across my bare arm, "Look here baby girl if you ever need anything, you just come by and see old Moe. Cause I

can love you better than yo mama! Girl, I could make you scream into next year."
He laughed, stuck out his tongue and flashed a big wide grin so that I could see
all of his gold crowned teeth. I flinched in disgust.

I left Moe's apartment feeling like I needed to shower. I felt grimy and cheap,
and I wanted to rid myself of the smell of Moe's apartment building, and the
images of the dirty little girls, that seemed to linger in my mind, long after I left.

I used the navigator in the car to find my way around the city. My first stop
was to Elite Bail Bond where I posted bond for Justin.

The walk from the car to the bail bond office was long. Just checking out the
surroundings made me feel as if I were about to embark upon some new and
ominous territory.

I entered the office only to find that business was conducted from behind a
bulletproof glass. I guess they didn't trust the clientele.

The bondsman wore a shoulder holster with a gun inside. "Can I help you?"
"Hello I am here to post bond for Justin Black." The bondsman looked at me
and shook his head in pity.

"Yeah we got the call. You know I've got a daughter about your age and she's
pretty, just like you. Didn't anyone tell you this is a dangerous business? I hope
you know what you're doing."

"Thanks sir, but I'm okay."

The truth was that I wasn't okay, and I didn't have a clue as to what I was
doing!

As I turned the key in the ignition of my grandmother's car, I wondered why
no one had bothered to tell me how to deal with street people. Why hadn't my
parents taught me how to deal with this sub-culture of people, who excelled in
the arena of manipulating and using people? Why didn't I say no to Moe? I knew
how to say no to drugs but not to Justin or Moe. Maybe my college will offer a
course in 'street dynamics'.

Nicky

I drove to Silver Spring parked Diamond's Mercedes S500 and proceeded to walk
quickly up Wayne Avenue to the residence of a Miss Nicky Simms. I rang the
bell and waited.

A young woman in her early twenties answered the door. She was dressed very trendy in an orange chiffon backless dress, with orange and white sandals. I should admit that I was slightly intimidated because she was several inches taller than me, and coupled with the fact that she looked like a video vixen.

She looked me up and down and said, "So you're Justin's new trick."

I responded on point, "My name is Erica, and I am nobody's trick!"

"You don't need to get cute with me Missy. I was his woman first and I'm the mother of his baby."

I must have looked perplexed because Nicky went on to say "Yeah, that's right, he my baby's Daddy."

Nicky was the mother of Justin's son, Joe. Joe held tight to his mother's leg while she talked to me. Joe was cutest little bright-eyed boy that I'd ever seen. I wondered why Justin hadn't mentioned that he had a son.

"Look, I just need to drop off this package." I tried to sound older and tough, like a street girl: sort of like the girls I'd seen in the movies.

I handed her the package that Moe had given me and turned to walk away.

"Wait a minute Miss Thang! Let me make sure that everything is everything! I wanna make sure that your little ass didn't clip me."

I could not fathom what Nicky just said to me, "Clip you? You can't be for real."

"You better believe that I'm for real. Come in for a minute so I can handle my business in private. By the way, are you driving that Benz in front of my door?"

In my most snobby voice and with my nose in the air I answered "Yes I am."

She was real pissed as she blurted out "OU OU! Girl, I know he didn't buy that Benz for yo little ass, and I'm still driving a jeep. Let me find out! You just wait till I see him!"

I didn't bother to answer her. I just wanted to finish this business and be gone.

Nicky's condo was warm and inviting. It had lots of original art work: sculptures, oils and etchings. The furniture was fifties motif, with a few vintage reproductions. Somehow this Nicky person didn't go with the décor. She was outwardly beautiful but her demeanor was rotten and distasteful. I wondered what kind of a mother she was to Joe and what had Justin seen in her?

I walked over to look at a picture on the table. It was a picture of Justin, Nicky and Joe, one big happy family. It hit me like a ton of bricks, and I asked myself what the hell was I doing here? I felt stupid!

Nicky opened the package with a knife. There were three sandwich bags full of dope. I was paralyzed with shock when I realized that I'd been asked to transport drugs. Nicky saw the expression on my face and realized that I had no idea of what I was doing.

"Pretty girl, you really are green."

I felt like I was going to throw-up.

"Where's your bathroom?"

Nicky allowed me to use her bathroom, and I emptied the contents of my stomach into her toilet.

When I came out of the bathroom Nicky was different. Her short curly hair framed her pretty face and she was no longer using street vernacular. Her posture had changed and except for the outrageous nails, the ten gold chains and twenty gold bracelets, she seemed like one of the girls from back home. She even gave me a glass of water and asked me to sit down for a minute.

We talked for nearly an hour, mostly about Justin and the last 24 hours.

Nicky said, "So tell me about your relationship with Justin?"

"There isn't much to tell. I just met him two days ago. I thought he was a nice guy but I guess I was wrong."

"I am going to ask you something and I want you to be honest with me. Did he hit it?"

"Do you mean did we have sex?"

"Damn girl you can't be that naïve. Yeah, that's what I mean."

"No we haven't had sex?"

Nicky was relieved to know that Justin and I weren't sleeping together. She smiled a rather wicked smile, as if she'd gained some instant confidence and assumed some self-respect, from knowing that Justin and I hadn't made love.

She went on to say, "Girl if I were you, I wouldn't give him the time of day. Look at how he used you."

I think Nicky was so blinded by her love for Justin that she didn't realized that she was being used as well.

I asked her, "What about your baby? Don't you think that your life style will affect him?"

Nicky stared at the floor as if looking for the right thing to say. "When he gets old enough to understand, I will probably get out of the life or send him to live with my aunt in North Carolina."

Nicky was from Durham, North Carolina: a small town girl who was trying to make it in the big city. She conveyed to me how she'd met Justin at Howard in their freshman year and how Joe was born at the end of her junior year. She'd started school on a four-year scholarship but lost it when she didn't return for her senior year. Both Justin and she had plans to go back to school but the money and the bling-bling was too good to give up right now.

She said Justin broke up with her right after Joe was born but he continued to spend every Thursday and Saturday night with her and he allowed her to handle his financial affairs. She knew he had other women but she loved him no matter what! After all he was her baby's daddy.

Nicky spent her days intercepting drugs and money, and watching soaps. Her nights were spent in the clubs trying to keep up with Justin. Nicky was a beautiful young woman with lots of potential but she'd given up on ever being anything but Justin's doormat! Despite the fact that Justin Black AKA Slick was a liar, a cheat and a drug-dealer, she loved him and believed in him.

I hated Justin Black because he was the worst kind of womanizer. He was a smooth talker with good looks: using his charm to lure naïve young women to help him in his drug operation.

As I turned to leave, Nicky handed me an envelope with my name on it. I opened it and counted five thousand dollars in cash. I was shocked and I honestly tried to give the money back but she refused it, saying that I earned it, and that she would get into trouble with Justin if she didn't give it to me.

"Listen up baby girl, you earned these dollars."

Then she smiled and said, "Just don't ever let me catch your ass with my man."

I didn't know if I should to say thanks for the money, give her a hug, or just leave.

As I turned to leave, I patted Little Joe on the head, and said good luck to Nicky.

Later that evening Meagan called me to say she ran into Justin at the mall and that he'd made bail and he wanted to see me. I knew that he was trying to get in touch with me because his number kept appearing on my caller ID all afternoon, but I refused to answer. I told Meagan to tell him that I was leaving for the west coast in the morning.

"Erica he is so fine, how can you refuse to see him? He has women standing in line to be with him!" For that moment I thought of Justin, with his big brown eyes, smooth chocolate skin, and his incredible body. I thought of the affect that his perfectly cut body had on the clothes that he wore. I remembered the dance and the sweet kiss but somehow the realization of how little value he'd placed on my life, by involving me in his drug world, suddenly made my feelings for him diminish to zero.

I told Meagan about Moe and Nicky but to my surprise, she said that she wished she could have made 'five grand' that easy. It didn't faze her in the least about what could have happened to me. She asked, "If you're really finished with him, do you mind if I have a go at him?"

What a bitch she turned out to be. I asked her, "Do you think he'll want you? I mean after all he knew you first, so he had an opportunity to go after you if he wanted you."

"Sounds like you might be a little jealous."

I was jealous. A little more than twenty-four hours ago I thought I was passionately in love with Justin. Even though I hated him, the thought of him with Meagan made me angry. She was nothing more than an opportunist, just like Diamond said.

She antagonistically said, "I'll be his trophy. A man like that needs a trophy woman."

Now I was really mad. "He has a trophy girl and a little boy and besides why would you want to get involved with a drug-dealer."

"Erica you've got a lot to learn about life. Unlike yourself, I don't have a rich grandmother, I need money and if I can get some cash as easy as you did, I want the job."

"What you're saying is that you're willing to be his drug-runner for a few lousy dollars."

"Where I come from five thousand dollars is a lot of money."

I guess Diamond was a better judge of character than I thought. Meagan was absolutely the worst human being that I'd ever met. She didn't care about me and even less about herself.

Later in the week Meagan called to say that they were trying to raise money to help Sean get out of jail, before his family found out, and if I could help. As much as I wanted to help, I wanted nothing to do with the drug scene or its players.

Pretty boy Sean had been sexually assaulted by two men while in the bullpen and was now on suicide watch at the jail. It was painful to hear about Sean. It must have been awful having one man force himself in your mouth, while simultaneously another man rips open your rectum, and all time your best friend and others stand by and do nothing to help you.

Sean, a pre-med student with a promising future was in jail waiting a grand jury indictment and too ashamed to call his parents for help.

Sean Charles Wyndham, III grew up in the lap of luxury. He was what you'd call old money. He was a sheltered boarding school student from Hartsdale, New York. He'd come to Georgetown University with dreams of becoming a surgeon, like his father, and his father before him. He was destined to be the third generation doctor in his family but with a drug conviction hanging over his head, it wasn't likely to happen.

I guess the 'bad boy' image wasn't worth it after all.

I wished I could've helped him but I didn't have a clue as to what I could do, without having to deal with Justin. Anyway, why should I get involved? After all Sean was an adult who had choices. It seemed so strange, that with his good looks and obvious intelligence, he was content to be a pawn in Justin's game.

7

WBIT FM

Shanae Bugatch was one of the interns at the station. She was a rising senior at Spellman College who got an internship every summer because of her excellent scholastic record of 4.0. She was witty, cute, and personable. Diamond said she had real leadership ability and that's why she appointed her my mentor for the summer.

Shanae and I hit it off as lunch partners' right from the start. Today she said she wanted to pull me up about something she'd heard.
"I heard that you've been hanging out with Meagan. Please say it isn't so."
I was caught off guard, "What do you mean? What did you hear?"
I wondered what she heard. I'd hoped that this Justin business would not get back to Diamond.
"I heard that you've been hanging in bad company."
"I don't know what you're talking about."
"Okay, I'll just say it in plain English because whispers have been flying and I know that you don't want any of this to get back to Diamond."

I'd managed to keep everything from Diamond up to this point and the thought of her finding out that I'd behaved irresponsibly was upsetting.
"Have you been seeing a guy named Slick and did Meagan turn you on to him?"
Trying desperately to sound innocent I said, "Oh do you mean Justin Black, the junior at Howard University? Yes, I met him when I was out with Meagan one night."
"Cut the crap Erica! I am here to let you know that it was not a by chance meeting. You were being recruited to run drugs for Justin."
"I don't know what you're talking about."

42

I could not believe what I was hearing. How could this be possible? I thought Justin was sincerely attracted to me and that I'd just happened to come on the scene at a bad time in his life. Shanae must be mistaken because this kind of thing only happened to a certain kind of girl, not to girls like me.

"Did you know that Meagan recruits young naïve women to help Justin run his drug operation? Don't lie to me Erica because Sheila the temp from human resources happened to see you with him at the mall."

My stomach was in knots as I thought about Diamond, my grandmother who was so proud of me. What if this got back to her?

"Meagan uses drugs?" My mouth was wide open.

"Close your mouth and open your eyes and stay away from Meagan and Justin."

Things were finally beginning to make sense. So this was the reason why Meagan was so dead set on me getting back with Justin. She'd even tried to make me jealous.

I asked Shanae in my most humble voice, "Did you say anything to Diamond?"

"No and I won't, not unless I hear that you are still hanging out with Meagan and Justin!"

I felt relieved, "So this is our little secret."

"This is will be our secret to the grave unless you renege."

I gave Shanae a big hug, and thanked her for looking out for me.

Later on in the week Meagan showed up at the station wearing very dark shades but her shades could not hide the black and blue marks under her left eye. Her lime green and pink designer shirt looked less than fresh and her milky white face was red and splotchy. I politely asked her what she wanted.

"What's up Meagan?"

She started fidgeting with her bracelet, asking if she could borrow some money because she needed to go home.

"I need to borrow some money for my trip back home."

I answered, "Don't your classes start in a couple of weeks?"

"Yes, but I need to go home to tie up some business and to see my mum."

"I'm sorry but I can't help you."

"You've got to help me. I don't have anyone else to turn to. Do you still have the five grand that Justin gave you?"

"No, I bought a couple of designer outfits and it's all gone."

"All of it?

I nodded yes.

"How could you spend five grand on a couple of outfits?"

I told her that where I come from five thousand dollars was not a hell of a lot to spend on two complete outfits: shoes and bags included. I thought of the last time my mother and I went shopping, and we met with her personal shopper. By the time we left the store, my Mom had spent close to fifteen thousand dollars on two outfits and matching accessories.

Meagan looked as desperate as she sounded. She even asked me to pawn my Piaget watch.

"Let me borrow your watch. I promise I'll get it back to you in a couple of weeks."

I was beginning to feel overpowered, so I asked her to wait a minute. When I returned, it was with my friend Shanae. Meagan looked upset that I was with Shanae and she was definitely caught off guard.

Shanae in her cool and sophisticated voice asked, "Meagan my good friend, what's up?"

"Nothing girl, I just stopped by to say hello to Erica but I would like to speak to her in private."

Shanae spoke very authoritatively, "Anything that you have to say to her you can say to me."

Meagan was infuriated. I could hear the anger in her voice as she looked in my direction.

"Hey Erica, you know me, so why are you tripping? You know how we go."

I looked her directly in the eyes, feeling confident with Shanae at my side, "No Meagan, I don't know how we go."

Shanae stepped in front of me saying, "Meagan whatever you're selling we ain't buying. And by the way Erica is hip to how you and Justin play the game. Now that you know, that we know, you can stop wasting our time. You need to take the nearest exit before I call security or even worse, tell your Uncle Sydney!"

Meagan turned and walked away with tears streaming from under her dark glasses and for a moment, I almost felt sorry for her.

The next day at lunch Shanae told me that I was one among many of the young woman that Meagan recruited for Justin. Luckily, most of the girls had managed to escape unscathed. I asked Shanae if Sydney knew about his precious niece. She assured me that he didn't have a clue.

"Someone needs to tell him."

"Erica, I know how you feel but if you put her out there, you risk Diamond finding out about your involvement with them. Trust me, it will all catch up with her, and sooner than you think."

8

Meagan and Moe

Meagan was desperate because she'd stolen and misused close to $25,000 in drugs that belonged to Justin. He'd given her a deadline to pay him back and her black eye was his signature from one of his enforcers. Meagan knew that it was impossible to raise the money, so she asked Justin to let her work it off. Her first job was to spend a week playing wifey to old Moe. Moe in return was going to knock $5000.00 off the debt. After all, the money that she owed Justin was really his.

On Meagan's first night with Moe, he was so happy to have her, that he took her uptown to dinner, to show her off to his associates but Meagan's face showed that she wanted to be anywhere other than with him. Moe was trying hard to treat her well and he was really proud of her.

"Hey princess can I get you a drink."

She frowned and responded, "Why not."

"Well what will it be?"

"I'll have Moet."

It was rare for him to cater to a woman but he thought she was pretty and he wanted to please her, so he ordered a bottle without reservation. During the course of the evening he stepped up his game and attempted to engage her in intellectual conversation but she looked bored and even more irritated.

At one point he left the table to answer a call and when he got back Meagan sat with her back to him sipping his Champagne acting as if he were something insignificant.

When they arrived back at his place he told her to get undressed. Reluctantly she complied. When he'd had enough of her arrogance, he slapped her so hard that blood gushed from her nose and lip.

"Bitch don't you ever act as if you're ashamed of me. And don't let me have to remind you again, that for the next seven days I own you."

In excruciating pain and with tears streaming from her eyes she said, "Moe I'm sorry."

"Now get on your hands and knees and tell me you love me. Then I want you to beg me to make love to you." Meagan got down on her hands and knees.

She was hardly audible as she mumbled, "I love you Moe. Please make love to me, Moe."

Pretending not to hear her, he said, "What's that. I can't hear you."

"Moe I swear I love you."

"And what is it that you want me to do to you?"

"Please make love to me."

"Stop lying bitch and run my bath water."

The next evening they went to a club on Water Street. Meagan was wearing a beautiful black sequined designer dress and jacket, compliments of Moe's favorite booster. She looked absolutely stunning with her matching crystal accessories.

Everyone was watching the young attractive woman and the older man as they danced to Fat Joe's 'Lean Back". The song played twice. Moe appeared tired at the end of the dance and his feet hurt but he needed to keep up with Meagan for appearance sake. He breathed a silent sigh of relief when the dance ended. Pretending to be upbeat and happy, he struggled to make it back to his seat.

And now that he had everyone's attention he needed to show them who was in control, so he had Meagan get down on her knees and wipe his shoes while everyone watched. When she finished he told her to go to the bar and get the drinks "And don't stop to talk to anyone." On her way to the bar several young men asked her to dance but she kept her eyes on the floor, fearing for her life.

Meanwhile Moe was getting mad attention from the ladies. They thought he was either a millionaire or someone real important. Why else would someone like Meagan be out with him and catering to him? Before they left the club Moe had collected at least 10 or more phone numbers from some of the most beautiful girls that DC had to offer. When he thought about it Meagan had really given his self-esteem a boost!

Moe

Moses Johnson a well-known Kingpin from east Baltimore was middle-aged and broken from spending 25 years in Federal prison. At age 52, 20year old Meagan was just the boost that he needed to get back on the circuit. His friends needed to know that he still had it going on with the women.

He was a well-known O.G. in DC and Baltimore and the 'dope boys' who were trying to gain a rep respected him. For the moment he was laying low so as not to draw attention to himself, but he was still a major player in the drug world. In fact he was probably pulling in about 100 grand a week.

Before he was arrested, he owned a home in Phoenix, Maryland, a mini yacht and a Lamborghini. He knew what the good life was all about but for now he was content to live in squalor until he felt secure enough to stretch out.

Moe grew up in Baltimore City around Greenmount Avenue and 25th Street, a fairly integrated section of the city in the late 50's and 60's. By the time he was eighteen he'd slept with at least twenty-five women. Some of them even offered to make him their Pimp.

Clients knew his mother, as Fannie Blue Light. Fannie was exceptionally pretty, with waist long hair, delicate features, and an eighteen-inch waist. Her mother died when she was five, and she never knew her father, but her mean-spirited aunt and cousins with whom she lived: constantly reminded her that he was a white man.

In the spring of her senior year of high school her home economics teacher encouraged her to enter a beauty pageant. It was the summer of 1950 that a local cosmetic company at Carr's Beach in Baltimore crowned her beauty queen. This was the same summer that she met and married Moe's father.

Rob, who was five years her senior was employed by the local steel mill. From all outward appearances it appeared as if the two would have a good life together that is until he decided to flip the script.

Two years into the marriage Rob became sexually abusive of Fannie, basically because he thought that she was too pretty to be trusted. All day while he worked he envisioned her with other men and when he got home he made her pay for his fanaticizing. He would brutally rape her and afterwards expect her to fix dinner and want her to pretend that the rape never occurred. A few months into the second year of marriage Fannie left Rob. It was difficult at first because she had a baby to think of but she was determined not to return to her aunt's house. Her baby would never suffer the taunting and verbal abuse that she'd suffered at her aunt's house.

She found employment at Baltimore's famous 'Houses' Restaurant. Her good looks made her popular with the male patrons at the establishment. The men openly flirted with her in the presence of their wives and companions, placing their business cards in her hands, accompanied by large tips. After a couple of years of working twelve hour a day shifts at the 'white only' restaurant on Eastern Avenue, and with so little time to spend with Moe: she decided to go into business for herself. At the end of her first year of employment at the restaurant, she'd began dating a Greek business-man who moved her into her nice town house, furnishing all three floors with exquisite furniture.

When she began her scheme, she would purposely ask to wait the tables of the mayor, and the other elite clientele who frequented the restaurant. When she established a clientele of ten regulars, she quit her minimum wage job at the restaurant and made a lucrative living prostituting to the businessmen that she'd met at the restaurant. Before she resigned, she figured her new salary per week to be ten times the amount that she'd made at the restaurant in one week.

Moe never saw his mother's clients because she conducted her business on the weekends while Moe visited with his father and sometimes during the day while Moe was in school.

She acquired the name 'Fannie Blue Light' because she entertained her clientele in her basement under a blue light.

When Moe turned fifteen, his best friend Bruce told him that some of his friends were talking about his mother behind his back. In those days the code on the streets of East Baltimore was that you did not disrespect someone's mother. And you had to be crazy to disrespect Moe Johnson's mother because Moe was known for 'kicking ass and taking names'. Eventually, he caught up with his so-called friends, and one by one and beat them beyond an inch of their lives.

Although, he suspected what was going on he never confronted his mother and by the time he reached high school, she'd moved her business to an upscale apartment across town, employing several college girls to work for her. In all actuality he never had first hand knowledge of his mother's business.

Moe was at least 6 ft 2 with light brown eyes, a caramel complexion and a face that looked like it had been chiseled to resemble that of a Greek God. His naturally cut body, made him look as if he lived to workout. No woman could deny that Moe Johnson was 'most definitely' fine. At age eighteen his mother bought him a brand new red corvette for his birthday. With his good looks and new car he was easily the most popular kid in his neighborhood.

He graduated from Baltimore City College at the top of his class and attended Morgan State University on a track scholarship. During his sophomore year he started hustling on a small scale but it wasn't long before the notorious Little Tony recognized him as a leader. A few months after graduation, he gained his own territory and became 'top dog' on the Eastside.

At age twenty-five, Moe married Andrea, a naïve young woman from White Plains, New York, whom he met while a student at Morgan. The daughter of a prominent Yonkers' minister, she was pretty, smart and everything any man could have wanted but Moe could not resist abusing her. Although, the abuse was more mental rather than physical, it was still abuse. When Moe was angry he would get in her face and curse her until she cried.

One evening after Andrea and her friends had come from shopping they decided to stop at a club on Reisterstown Road for a drink. Andrea brought several bottles of champagne for her friends because she had something to celebrate. She'd found out this afternoon that she was six weeks pregnant. She sipped on a coke, while her girls sipped on Moet.

Her main girl Lisa inquired, "Have you told Moe?"

"No. I was waiting for the right time."

"This is the right time. You can't hide a thing like this from the father."

"He's not ready. I mean I'm not ready."

"What do you mean you're not ready? Don't you think he'll be happy about the baby?"

"I hope so but I can't be sure. Every time that I've even remotely mentioned the possibility of starting a family to him, he shuts down."

"Shutting down is the initial response for a lot of men when they are confronted with fatherhood but he's your husband! When do you plan to tell him?"

"I don't know. I guess I'm waiting for the right moment."

"Sooner or later you're going to have to tell him."

"Okay, I'll tell him tonight. I guess tonight is as good a time as any. I just hope he's in a good mood."

As chance would have it, one of Moe's workers was in the club, saw Andrea and gave Moe a call to tell him of her whereabouts. Andrea arrived home to find that Moe had scattered all of her belongings on the lawn. Hadn't he warned her about going in clubs where he transacted business? She knew that he was involved in a dangerous business and that she put them both at risk by hanging in the wrong places. Maybe this would teach her a lesson about not following his directions.

Although, Moe would probably apologize later and maybe even help her collect her belongings from the lawn, it was too late. Andrea took this opportunity to leave him. She could not imagine raising her child in this volatile atmosphere. When she was sure that he'd left the house, she gathered her things and retreated to upstate New York to live with relatives until she was able to make it on her own. In the year that followed Moe searched everywhere for her but he never saw her again.

In the days that followed he became increasingly bitter and angry at the irretrievable loss of his wife. His anger eventually began to cloud his judgment and it ultimately resulted in his incarceration.

Years later while incarcerated, he would learn through intense therapy that he could not respect women because of how he secretly viewed his mother. He did not respect, nor did he trust women and as far as he was concerned, they were just pawns in his game.

Meagan and Moe went out every night for the week that she lived with him. On her last night he mixed her hit with cocaine and heroine. He was hoping to hook her, so that she would be his forever, and it worked like a charm. Moe could depend on Meagan stopping by everyday for a hit or two.

Within a months' time the two moved uptown to a swank condo on Capitol Hill. Moe got his self-esteem back and Meagan was happy to have her habit fed.

9

Why Me?

Diamond was smart, sexy and sophisticated with a dynamic personality. She got her start with the production of one syndicated radio talk show. In five years she owned six stations on the east coast. Breaking rank with the competitive stations, her stations targeted a wide range of listeners, from soft rock to Hip-Hop, Pop to R and B. I admired my grandmother and hoped to be just like her one day.

In the days that followed Diamond made me feel more than special. I felt that special kind of love that only exits between a grandparent and grandchild. She assigned me to the position of intern at the station and no matter what she'd planned for the workday she always found time to have lunch with me. After work we did everything together, the gym, dinner engagements and even the boring client meetings.

On Thursday evenings Diamond dined at 'Bottoms Up', one of the swankest restaurants in the nation's capital. Diamond said it was good for business to eat there because the 'who's who' in DC ate there.

On this Thursday night, I was supposed to meet her best friend, Judge Burton Hatcher. However, he called to say that he could not make it because of a prior engagement.

Halfway through dinner, the maitre d' paged Diamond. She kissed me on the forehead and left the table. A few minutes later a waiter came to the table, and told me to gather my things as well as my grandmother's and to come with him.

I made my way through the crowd to find that Diamond fainted. A crowd of people stood around her as she was helped from the floor to the chair. I pushed through the crowd asking, "Grandmother, what happened?" Diamond could hardly speak but she managed to say, "Erica, I need you to call Sidney and tell him to pick us up."

"Why can't I drive?"

"Erica call, Sidney! Please don't ask me anything else! I'll explain when we get home."

By the time Sidney arrived Diamond looked physically ill. Her lipstick was smudged and her blouse hung on the outside of her skirt.

Everyone was silent on the ride home. Sydney pulled into the driveway and escorted us into the house. Diamond appeared to be in a daze. Reagan and Christen, Diamond's two best friends arrived a few minutes after us.

Reagan told Diamond, "Girl my heart hurts for you. I am so very sorry. Please tell me what needs to be done."

Christen gave Diamond a big hug and Diamond broke down in tears. "Diamond I am so sorry. I've got my overnight bag in the car, so if you don't mind I like to stay here with you, tonight."

Diamond nodded yes.

I was clueless about what was going on and it seemed no one knew what to say to me. I was being avoided.

Diamond asked everyone to go to another room because she needed to be alone with me.

I wondered if something really bad had happened at the station, or if Diamond found out that she was terminally ill, after-all, she did go to the doctor yesterday. No she couldn't be sick because we were having such a good time. Please God don't let her be sick!

"Erica there's been an accident."

"Accident?"

Miles and Carmen were in a plane crash."

Suddenly, I couldn't move. Words were spilling from my mouth but I was having an outer body experience.

"What plane crash? "Where are my mother and my father? Did my mother and father die?"

"Yes Erica they are gone." I wanted to die but I couldn't even cry. I must be a bad child because I couldn't cry. Diamond didn't cry either because it was all too unreal.

My mind began to think irrational thoughts. Someone must be confused because I spoke to Miles this morning and he told me that he and Carmen were taking a flight to Monaco in the afternoon. Maybe they survived the crash and hadn't been found yet or maybe they'd missed the flight. But Diamond said there were no survivors.

Maybe I was dreaming this horrific nightmare. It had to be a dream. This morning when I spoke with my father he told me that they'd taken a moonlight cruise on the Seine River last night. I wondered if they knew that it would be the last cruise they would ever take, or the last moonlight that they would ever see.

When I awakened the next day, reality set in and I was angry. How dare this happen to my parents? What did I do to deserve this? My beautiful parents were gone forever from my life. The thought of it made me sick. At this moment, I longed to smell my mother's sweet perfume and to feel my father's strong embrace.

Why was God punishing me? I became angry and wished it had been someone else's parents rather than mine.

Why me? Why did they have to go? What was the purpose? Who made the decision? Could the decision be reversed?

I should have gone with them. If I had gone with them, the three of us would be together. I didn't want to live without them. Why should I live? What purpose did my life have now? I was angry. It wasn't fair. I prayed to God to bring them back, promising him that I would be good for the rest of my life.

The nights turned into days. I couldn't sleep and I couldn't eat. I floated through time like an observer rather than actually being there.

People were constantly in and out of Diamond's house, offering their condolences.

I found it easier to nod my head rather than to talk.

10

Saying Goodbye

A week passed, and Diamond said it was time to plan the memorial service for Miles and Carmen. That meant we would have to go to California. Beautiful southern California, the only home I'd ever known, now seemed like a dream of long ago.

Reagan and Christen were on the scene being attentive to Diamond's every whim. As for me, I missed my best fiend Kennedy. I longed to sit face to face with her and tell her everything that I was feeling. I wondered if she would understand about the visions of my parents that I constantly had. Would she understand that they came to me in a dream to tell me that they were okay and that one-day I would be with them? Or would she think I was crazy?

We arrived in L.A. on a hot August afternoon. Adrian, my maternal grand-mother, greeted us at the airport: insisting that we stay with her. But Diamond insisted that we stay at my parent's house. Diamond said we needed time to reflect among Miles and Carmen's things.

Adrian Bovier-Duvalier, my maternal grandmother was a Louisiana Creole. I guess you could say that she had an upper middle class upbringing because her family owned quite a bit of land and a few business ventures in Louisiana. Her husband, and my grandpapa, Dr. Reynard Claude Fresnel, a Haitian born immi-grant grew up in impoverished Haiti, but managed to attend medical school, graduating at the top of his class. It was often commented that he possessed the 'the island man mystic', and that he was a real lady-killer. Adrian the dutiful wife closed her eyes to her husband's many infidelities and concentrated on the lives of her six children. Although Adrian was considered a class act, she was not Dia-mond. Diamond was a high-powered executive type while Adrian was content to walk in her husband's shadow.

These two beautiful ladies who rarely talked to each other must now come together in a common bond of memorializing their children.

I thought, "What will become of me?" I was an orphan. What would my future be? What about high school and my friends?

Diamond said everything regarding the memorial service must be done in the best of taste and with dignity. Death had not diminished the love that this mother had for her son. Her son deserved the best even in death.

There were a million things to do to prepare for guests, and the list became longer and longer.

My home, once featured in 'Best Homes Magazine', now seemed empty and lifeless.
I called Tina the housekeeper to come and prepare the house for guests.

That night as I lay tossing and turning in my bed, I was awakened several times by what sounded like laughter, and intimate sounds coming from my parent's room. I walked across the hall to their room and for a split second I saw Miles and Carmen lying in bed embracing each other. They were so into each other that they did not see me but as I came closer to the bed they disappeared. I jumped up on the bed and stood screaming and crying for them to come back and take me with them. Diamond came in and beckoned for me to come down from the bed. She said that I was dreaming. We went down to the kitchen where she brewed some chamomile tea and held me until I calmed down.

The next morning my friends and my parent's friends began to fill the house.
It felt good to know that so many people cared. I looked across the room at my friend Madison and for a split second I wished it had been her parents instead of mine. After all, her parents fought all the time and never had time for Madison or her brother. Once her dad came to our school reeking of liquor and her mother always looked like a hooker. It just didn't seem fair that my good parents were gone, and her awful parents were still here. And what about Kennedy's parents? They were old. She even said that that they were too old to be her parents! I wished I could make a deal with God to make an exchange. I was miserable and I wanted God and the world to know it.

Later in the afternoon my friends Madison and Kennedy, drove me to the hair salon. For some reason my hair and nails seemed insignificant during this time in my life but my friends made sure that I didn't let my appearance go.

Everyone thought I should try to be as normal as possible. But what is normal? Normal would be having my parent's undivided attention at the dinner table or going shopping with my mother. Being an only child would make one think that I was intrinsically lonely but that was not the case. My parents were apart of everything that I did and I loved it that way. I shared everything with them as one would a best friend. I would give anything just to go to the grocery store with my Mom: a chore that I normally hated, would now be a blessing. It's funny how all of the insignificant things now appeared paramount. I wondered if I would ever be normal again. I prayed that God would help me feel normal or let me die!

The memorial service was beautiful. Diamond maintained her composure throughout the service. I sat on one side of Diamond and there was an empty seat on the other side of her.

Halfway through the service we were joined by a tall man with a long braid that extended halfway down his back. The man wept openly. It was Grandpa Clayton! I had not seen him for more than six years. It had been six years since the last time that we visited the reservation as a family. My dad on the other hand visited with his family on the reservation every summer, for one week. My mother hated the reservation with its primitive customs: so consequently, we took a separate vacation at that time. Usually, mother and I took a cruise, or rented a villa on one of the sparsely populated islands in the Caribbean.

I had almost forgotten about Grandpa Clayton. I was so glad to see him. He looked strong and handsome like my Dad. He and Diamond held hands throughout the service. The funny thing is that from that moment on he and Diamond connected so well, almost as if they had never been separated.

The service was beautiful but very long. When it was over there was a catered luncheon for family and friends at my house. Everyone was nice but I didn't feel any better. I fell asleep in a chair while talking to Kennedy and the next thing that I remembered was Grandpa Clayton carrying me upstairs to my room. He covered me with a blanket and kissed me on my forehead.

When I awakened the next morning, Diamond was calling me to breakfast. I went downstairs to find Diamond and Grandpa Clayton fully dressed and sitting on the veranda. I was glad that Diamond and Grandpa Clayton were together because they really needed each other. After breakfast I made the excuse that I needed to go shopping for a few things because I wanted them to have time alone: and besides, I needed to get away from everything that reminded me of the past.

As I drove into Beverly Hills, I thought what would become of me? Would Diamond take me in? Or was I just something for her to play with this summer! Maybe I would go to live on the reservation with Grandpa Clayton? It might be fun living on the reservation but God forbid I should have to live with my mother's parents. Grandpapa Dr. Fresnel was too domineering and too strict. I could never follow all of his rules and Grandmother Adrian would never have the guts to speak up for me. They were devout Jehovah's Witness and I was A.M.E. Would I have to knock on doors to earn my keep? I made up my mind, that if I had to live with them, I would run away.

And what if I had to move away to another city? What about all of my hard work at school? If I went to another high school in my senior year, colleges would look at me differently. It wouldn't matter that I was the president of the 'Debate Team' and the vice-president of the Student Government. I would be completely anonymous, if I went anywhere else for my senior year!

A few days after the memorial service my grandparents met with my attorney to discuss my future. Both the Redfern's and the Fresnel's argued over my fate. I couldn't believe how much my grandparents on both sides wanted me. It was the first time I saw Grandpa Fresnel become emotional to the point that tears streamed down his face. I think I reminded him of my mother, the daughter he loved more than anything.

Grandpa Fresnel in his very stern voice said, "I think the best thing for Erica is to come and live with us. After all, Adrian and I can provide her with a stable environment, a two parent home."

Adrian chimed in, "Yes, my husband is correct. Erica will need stability more than anything else now that her parents are gone. Reynald and I can offer Erica a loving and stable home."

At this point Diamond excused herself from the meeting and asked Clayton to speak with her in private. When they walked back into the room Diamond looked confident as she spoke very candidly about my future. "Erica has had enough turmoil in her life and we feel that she should not be forced to leave the comfort of the only home that she has ever known."

The Fresnels' continued to argue their point but they were no match for Diamond and Clayton.

At the end of the day it was decided that I would complete my senior year of high school in California. The agreement was that if Grandpa Clayton's company would allow him to transfer to LA, he would live in my house with me to make sure that I was properly supervised and Diamond would spend one weekend a month with us, until it was time for me to move east for college. More than anything, I was happy that Diamond really wanted me!

My trust fund had been set up in the amount of 2.5 million dollars and my assets totaled nearly as much. Money was not going to be a problem and I could go to the college of my choice.

With the summer finally over, it was time to get serious about school again. I wondered if I would ever be the same again. I tried to read a few scholarly pieces but my mind continued to drift back to happier times, like when my parents were still alive. Boy was I glad that I'd already taken my SATs because I couldn't concentrate on anything!

My friends, Kennedy and Madison were always around but they had no idea about how I felt, and I didn't want to talk to them about the death of my parents. Frankly, I was jealous because they still had their parents.

The first day of school was the hardest. This was the first time that I wished that I were invisible. I knew that the teachers and students meant well, with all of their verbal condolences but I wasn't ready to talk to them. I was tired of hearing them say, "I know how you feel because I lost my grandmother, my dog, my boyfriend". Why couldn't they understand that nothing that they'd lost compared to what I lost.

Diamond said that we needed grief counseling to get us through.

The three of us went to grief counseling. Diamond actively participated while Grandpa Clayton and I listened. After listening to some of the stories that were told in the meeting about the tragedies that these people had suffered, some how I felt better. Not in the sense that I was glad that they were suffering but because I didn't feel alone in my suffering. I began to realize that death is a part of life and that some day death would knock at my door but until that time, I should try to be the best person that I can be.

Carl and I ended up in the same English and Physics classes. I avoided making eye contact with him but each day he waited patiently at the end of class just to walk me to another class. When we walked I kept my eyes fastened to the floor, trying desperately not to make eye contact. In my mind I thought that if we made serious eye contact he would somehow know about Justin. He talked and I listened. Reluctantly, I agreed to go to the prom with him. He was too easy! Why didn't he make a fuss about why I never returned his calls? I would have felt better if he'd been angry.

I kept comparing Carl to Justin. Carl had classic good looks but Justin had sex appeal. Justin was a take-charge kind of man while Carl was content to let me take the lead. I wished I could forget about Justin. Maybe it was just unfulfilled infatuation but for some reason I couldn't let it go. I told myself, I would never again become involved with the likes of Justin Black but I would love to meet a man of good character who looked like him.

11

Back to Life, Back to Reality

Diamond took a red-eye flight home. She settled back in her seat and tried to reflect on the last month and a half, with all of its traumatic events.

Diamond was experiencing the nightmare that every parent fears: losing a child. She'd lost the dearest and most precious thing in her world, her son: her only child. She knew that Miles genuinely loved her and that he was proud of her, and she felt equally the same about him. Whenever he was in DC on business, he'd spend all of his leisure time with her. Her thoughts drifted back to Miles' terrible two's and how she protected him from playing in the toilet and with electrical sockets. How would she manage life without her son? She felt empty. She'd read in a self-help book that some parents have thoughts of suicide when they experience the loss of a child. For what real reason did a parent have for living when their child was gone? Others learned to cope by resorting to drugs and alcohol. Although she'd gained a granddaughter and rekindled the flame with her ex-husband, she would never again be complete.

Diamond walked into her office at 8: a.m. and was inundated with email and phone messages. She tried to arrange things in order of priority but it was difficult to concentrate. Her son's death was still very fresh but she knew that she needed to return to work to take her mind off of it.

There was an urgent message from Judge Burton Hatcher. He wanted to have dinner with her as soon as she returned. Burton had been her constant companion for the past five years. He'd always been attentive to her and a very good friend but she didn't love him. At least she told herself that she didn't love him.

It was he who filled her house with flowers when her son passed, and he stopped by every evening to check on her. He'd even taken care of the flight arrangements and the tickets to California for the memorial service.

One night in late spring of last year, they sat on the terrace of his penthouse condo in Bethesda, sipping champagne and listening to 'Incognito'. Diamond looked exceptionally beautiful on this night. Her hair was neatly pulled back to expose her delicate features. She wore a white linen pantsuit that complemented her beautiful bronze complexion while the moonlight enhanced her exquisiteness. For Burton the time was right and he produced a three-carat diamond ring from his pocket, setting it on the table in front of them. After a few glasses of champagne, Diamond agreed to marry him but she recanted her agreement the next morning, blaming it on too much champagne. Yet, he still continued to hang-on.

She'd never fallen in love with any man since Clayton but when Miles passed she felt so low that if Burton asked her to marry him at that moment she would have. And why not? He sincerely loved her and he had prominence in DC society. As a former federal prosecutor and now a Judge, he'd made a name for himself in Maryland Government.

Burton was a real looker, 6 ft 2, with a deep rich chocolate complexion and very masculine features. He possessed a voice quality that would make most women melt at the sound of it, and at forty-eight he had the body of a fitness instructor. Burton Hatcher was as smooth as silk.

They met at a charity fundraiser. For Burton the courtship was unforgettable, and one that he would cherish for the rest of his life, even though he was resigned to the fact that he could not have her completely. He knew that he could not fill the hole in her heart no matter how hard he tried but he continued to lavish her with expensive gifts, trips to Europe and fine dining: with the hope that one day he would win her over completely.

On their first date they attended a Broadway musical that Diamond had been dying to see, August Wilson's "Ma Rainey's Black Bottom".

On a blustery winter afternoon they caught the train to New York after work. They laughed and made small talk, and held hands as they walked along 42nd

Street, to the theater. Afterwards they took a limo to Harlem for a late night dinner at Sylvia's. When Diamond agreed to stay over night he was elated, but at the end of the day, he rented two rooms at the Waldorf. After an early morning breakfast they took a carriage ride thru central park before taking the train back to D.C.

Diamond called Burton and agreed to have dinner with him tonight: after all he deserved to know what her plans were. She didn't want to let him go completely but he needed to know that she was involved with Clayton. She mused, "How do you tell some one who loves you more than anything else in the world that it's over? How will he handle it? What will he think of me?" How will he handle it? Could they still be friends? She wanted his friendship.

Ebony, Diamond's secretary, interrupted her thoughts and informed her that Sydney was on the phone with an urgent matter. Meagan had been missing for weeks and no one seemed to know of her whereabouts.

"Hello Diamond."

"Yes Sydney what is it."

Sydney spoke very rapidly: his voice breaking in despair, "Diamond, its Meagan, my niece. She's been missing for weeks. She left a note to say that she was going to New York to visit some friends, but I've checked, and no one has seen her. I hate to bother you but I need some advice".
"Don't ever think that you are bothering me. You are family to me. Do you think that it's possible that she may have gone home to England?"
He sounded frantic, "No she didn't have any money, and besides I spoke to her mother this morning, and she hasn't heard from her in over a month."

"We can discuss this over lunch today. Make sure that you have everything written down and a recent photo of Meagan and I'll put someone on it right away."

"There is one more thing."
"What is it?"
"Do you think that Miss Erica may know of her whereabouts?"

"Well there is only one way to find out. I'll call tonight and ask her."

It was one of those evening's when Grandpa Clayton would be coming home later than usual. He'd either gone to the gym or he was volunteering at the Indian Center. I'd kicked back, watching one of those old Joan Crawford flicks, munching on salsa and chips. I enjoyed looking at the clothes that the old stars wore, rather than listening to the dialogue.

The phone rang. It was Diamond on the other end.

"Hello Erica. How are you?"

Half listening and watching the movie I responded, "I'm well thank you."

"Erica what I'm about to ask you is very serious. I need you to tell me the last time that you either talked to or heard from Meagan?

My heart skipped a beat as I tried to gather my thoughts. I wanted to lie but I couldn't.

"The last time I saw her was a month ago at the station."

"Why was she there? Who did she come to see?"

"She came to see me."

"Why? What did she want? I thought you'd stop going out with her."

"I did. She was there to borrow money."

"Did she say what she needed money for?"

"She said she needed it to go home."

"Did you give her any money?"

"No."

"Erica, I need you to make a list of all of her friends: at least the ones that you met."

"I don't understand. Why are you calling me about her? We only went out a couple of times."

I was nervous. Why was Diamond questioning me about Meagan? I wanted to forget Meagan and everyone associated with her.

"Erica, Sydney is out of his mind with worry. He hasn't heard from Meagan in weeks. He just wants to know if you can help him find her."

Very sarcastically I answered, "How can I help him, I'm in California and he's in DC."
Diamond said, "Young lady, I'm not sure if I like your tone."

"I'm sorry. It's just that I don't like Meagan."

"I find that very interesting because I thought the two of you really hit it off. But for now I want you to put your feelings about her aside, and help us find her. Can you do that?"

I thought about everything that Meagan tried to involve me in, and I hated her. Why should I care if they found her? But Diamond was asking me, so I felt compelled to help. I also knew that I had to be careful because I didn't want Diamond to find out about Justin. So I decided to tell her about Moe. I made up a story that Meagan was dating Moe. As far as I was concerned Moe and Meagan were two of a kind. I hoped they both got arrested.
"I met a lot of her friends but I can only remember this older man named Moe."

Diamond said, "This is an excellent start. Tell me all about Moe. Where does he live?"
I gave Diamond the address of Moe's Apartment. I pretended that I'd waited in the car while Meagan went inside.

"Erica can you give me a description of this Moe person?"

"Yes. He is dirty and old with a big stomach that hangs over his belt. Oh yea, and he has green eyes." I gave the best description that I could of Moe. I told Diamond how disgusting he was with his gold teeth.

Diamond asked, "And you were able to see all of that while sitting in the car?"

For a moment I was caught off guard, "Yes, because he walked her back to the car and he was smiling and that's how I saw his gold teeth."

"How long did you wait in the car for Meagan?"

I wondered if I would survive Diamond's interrogation without breaking. "About twenty-five minutes."

"Erica, the neighborhood is drug infested. You could have been picked up for who knows what: or maybe even shot accidentally in a drive-by? Are you sure of the address?"

"I am one hundred per cent sure."

"Erica does Meagan use drugs?"
"Yes, I heard that she uses drugs and that's why I stopped hanging out with her."

"Did Meagan try to introduce you to drugs?"

"No someone told me that she uses."

"Who told you that she uses?"
It was getting deep, and I didn't know if I should mention Shanae but I really didn't have a choice.

"Shanae Bugatch. That's who told me."

"And just how would Shanae know? I wasn't aware that they were friends."

"They aren't friends. Shanae knows people who know her."

"So you guys maybe speculating about Meagan's drug use."

"No, I am sure that she uses."

"When I get back you and I are going to sit down, and I am going to teach you some valuable lessons about life. I told you that Meagan was not the kind of girl that you should be associating with but it is obvious that you needed to learn for yourself. Do you realize that your behavior was reckless and irresponsible? What if this Moe person is a drug-dealer? I can't understand his connection to Meagan, unless he is her supplier."

"I'm sorry and I promise it won't ever happen again."

"Stop it Erica! You're just saying what you think I want to hear."

The last thing that I wanted to do was to disappoint Diamond. I knew that she'd put all of her hopes and dreams into my future, especially now that my dad was gone. I prayed with all my heart that she wouldn't find out about my involvement with Justin and Moe.

12

the Celebrity Crack Head

When Diamond had all of the information that she needed to get the investigation started, she called on one of her best friends, police commissioner Kurt Stencil, to help her find Meagan. Kurt called in two of his best detectives and promised Diamond that they would find Meagan.

The detectives went to the address that I gave for Moe, only to find out that he'd moved more than a month ago. They went door to door in the building with Meagan's picture until they found one of the neighbors who recognized her. The woman told the detectives that Meagan lived at the apartment with Moe for a short time. She said she could not believe that such a beautiful young woman would take up with a man like Moe. She also said that she peeped through the slot in her door, and witnessed Moe making drug deals on more than one occasion.

Around the corner the detectives encountered a narcotic informant from the neighborhood who was more than willing to tell all that he knew about Moe for a few dollars, and couple vials of cocaine.

One of the detectives asked the junkie, "Hey, Tracey can you help us out?"

The informant answered very arrogantly, "Maybe. What you got for me?"

His response angered the detective, "Don't get cute dope-head just answer the question? Do you know a dealer named Moe Johnson who lives around the corner?"

Tracey asked, "What is it worth to you?"

The detective responded, "Same as usual." The same as usual meant a couple vials of cocaine and twenty dollars.

Tracey realizing that they were desperate for information asked, "Can't you do better than the usual?"

Detective Blue became impatient and threw Tracey up against the wall saying, "Look bitch just tell us what we want to know, or when we find him, we'll be sure to let him know that you snitched on him? Do you understand me?"

Tracey, weak from years of drug abuse, slid down the wall and onto the ground. Wearing his designer clothes of yesterday that were tattered and torn, he got up from the ground, brushed himself off and gave up all the information that the detectives needed to run a check on Moses Michael Johnson.

The informant Tracey Hill was once a renowned reporter for a major television station. Ten years ago, he became addicted to crack-cocaine. He fell from grace, losing his job, his home and eventually his family. Now he was a bitter crack-head/police informant, wanting to bring everyone down he could, who was in the game. Once in a while Moe would trust Tracey to stand on the corner, to pick up or deliver his product. After Moe found out who he was, he often taunted Tracey and called him a celebrity crack-head. Tracey had a special hatred for Moe, and it gave him great pleasure to help to bring him down.

Through this informant the detectives traced Moe to a private club uptown. They put twenty-four hour surveillance on his comings and goings and eventually found out where he lived.

13

Serendipity

Diamond, Reagan and Christen

The silence in her office was deafening as Diamond pondered over what to tell Burton. Glancing at the clock she noticed that she'd been tapping her pen on her desk for the past twenty minutes. There seemed to be only one thing to do, and that was to call an emergency girlfriend's meeting.

Diamond called her two best friends Christen and Reagan to meet her after work. The three always met when one of them faced a dilemma because they knew each other inside and out.

Christen, a lawyer, a divorcee and the mother of twin girls, was Diamond's confidant, not only in the arena of law, but with matters of the heart as well. Christen and Diamond had quite a few things in common. Both were first generation American citizens of parents born in Africa. Diamond parents were from Somalia and Christen's parents from Morocco
Both led privileged childhoods on Embassy Row in DC.

Reagan Winters, like Diamond, was a timeless beauty. She was an old school playette, who grew up in the Taft House projects in Harlem. She was the true native New Yorker, pretty, well dressed, fast-talking, and self-assured.

Reagan dated nationally and internationally, and she considered herself a connoisseur of fine men. There was Paulie from Italy, Charles from London, and David from Nigeria, and a host of locals. She was pretty, smart and funny, and for as much as men loved her: most women hated her, and for some reason she loved it that way.

She'd met Diamond twelve years ago, while shopping at the Printemps in Paris. Diamond stood in line ahead of her, in one of the designer shops. When Reagan recognized that Diamond was having some difficulty with the language, while trying to make a purchase, she voluntarily helped her. Reagan was so fluent in French that Diamond thought she was a native of France. The two struck up a conversation and met for cocktails later that evening. They connected as if they were sisters.

Once back in the states Reagan called Diamond and asked her to help her find a job in the nation's capitol. Diamond read her resume and decided that the station could use her expertise in the area of public relations. The next week she called Reagan and left a message, offering her a phenomenal salary. When Reagan heard the message she was in shock and disbelief. In fact she listened to the message three times before she actually believed it.

"Hello Reagan, I've checked out your references and I am in the midst of putting a package together for you too include a signing bonus and a buyout. Let me know if the salary is agreeable to you?"

Reagan returned the call to Diamond. "Ms. Redfern. I am calling to say that I would like to come to work for you."
"Skip the formality, and call me Diamond. Is the package agreeable to you?"
"Yes it is fine. What I mean is, I accept. I mean thank you!"
Damn she sounded like an idiot.
"How soon can you make the move?"
"How soon can I start?"
Diamond laughed, she liked the sound of eagerness in her voice. "To be honest with you, I needed someone yesterday."
With extreme enthusiasm Reagan said, "Thank you. Oh thank you so very much! Just give me a couple of weeks to tie up ends here in New York, and I'll be there on the first of the month."

"For the first month you are welcome to stay at our guest quarters until you find a place."
Diamond hired her with one ambition, that she would be an asset to the station: and that she was.

She was a dedicated worker and soon landed the position as Diamond's right hand at the station. Diamond depended heavily on her ability to manage the public relations aspect of the station.

That evening the girlfriends met at Diamond's house in the city after work. Both Christen and Reagan arrived ahead of Diamond.

"Chris you've got to help me with this. I don't know what to say to Burton. I don't want to lose his friendship but I need to tell him about Clayton. What do you think?"

"Diamond there is no easy way to say goodbye but are you sure that this is what you really want?

"That's the problem. I am not 100% sure of what I want."

Reagan commented, "I would be upfront with him, and drop his ass!"

Diamond thought, could this be the same woman that she'd hired twelve years ago. Where was the idealistic and the optimistic Reagan? Why had she become so bitter, and in some ways even distant?

"Reagan how can you be so cold, I thought you liked Burton."

"What does that have to do with anything? I am just saying what I would do if it were me."

"Reagan that is so heartless. Christen what do you think?"

Christen said, "I would weigh both of the relationships. You've been with Burton for more than five years and he has been great to you. Do you really want Clayton, or is this an illusion that maybe the result of you guys having lost your son?"

Diamond replied, "I can't be sure."

Reagan chimed in, "He can't be that great because she won't marry him.

Christen said, "Do you have to make up your mind tonight? Why not give yourself some time."

Diamond and Burton

Diamond met Burton for dinner at 'Bottom's Up'. The conversation was light and Burton could tell that she was far away. He assumed that she was thinking of the recent loss of her son. She'd barely touched her aesthetically and delicious meal, of veal medallions, topped with marinated greens and a Waldorf salad.

It was Burton who broke the ice, "How was your day?"

"It was great."

"Somehow I don't hear greatness in your voice."

"I suppose that I'm a little tired. Maybe I'm feeling delayed jet lag."

For Burton, it seemed as if Diamond had been gone for much longer than two weeks. He'd missed her more than she could ever imagine. He wondered why she wasn't feeling the bounce that he felt after this long period of separation. He wanted to get through dinner and take her back to his place, and maybe have her for dessert.

Most of the time he would hide his real feelings for her: pretending he was okay with her periods of indifference but tonight he wanted every part of her in his mouth.

After dinner, the two went to Burtons' place for a nightcap. Burton was hoping to inspire Diamond to spend the night. He'd filled the penthouse with white Iris, Diamond's favorite flower. The lights were dim and the mood was right for love.

He grabbed her around the waist from behind, and pulled her against him, whispering how much he'd missed her. The music, and the fire in the fireplace coupled with the big bulge in his pants would have melted the heart of the most indifferent lover, but Diamond made the excuse that she was facing an early morning meeting, and left.

Reagan, Burton and Diamond

The strong sun made a beautiful day in the nation's capitol. Although it was mid November, it felt like an Indian summer day. The temperature was about sixty-five degrees and the streets were full of tourists looking for the perfect place to have lunch. It was the kind of day that made life worthwhile.

Reagan strolled along Georgia Avenue in her five-inch heels and a black cashmere military style princess coat. Although, mentally exhausted from early morning appointments, she somehow managed to walk three blocks from the station, over to the District Court of Appeals and into Judge Burton Hatcher's Chambers.

She'd called ahead so that Burton was expecting her. Making her way through security, she finally reached his chambers.

Burton asked her to come in, and to sit for a moment while he prepared himself for court. He looked so regal and so handsome surrounded by the Judge's wood in his office.

"Burton it is so important that I talk to you."

While putting on his robe Burton answered, "I don't have much time. What's wrong?"

"It's about Diamond."

Unable to hide his concern for the woman he loved, Burton's voice dropped an octave when he asked, "What about Diamond? Is she okay?"

"Physically yes, emotionally no."

"Reagan I wish you would speak frankly, and get to the point. I have a very busy afternoon ahead."

"Burton it is so involved. What if I drop by your place around seven, and then I will tell you everything?"

He didn't have to tell her where he lived because Diamond entertained a few out of town guests at his place just last month, and she'd been invited.

"Seven sounds okay."

"I'll see you then."

Diamond stopped at Reagan's office around 4:30 to ask if they could go for drinks after work.

"Hey Reagan do you think that you could meet me at 'Fat Cat's' after work today?"

Diamond was the last person that she'd hoped to run into. She could hardly look her in the eye as she replied, "I am so sorry but I have the worst headache and cramps on top of that. Do you mind if I take a rain check?"

Diamond was perplexed because this was so unlike Reagan to turn down an invitation to happy hour.

"I understand. Anyhow, I should be packing to go to California for Thanksgiving."

Suddenly Reagan's thoughts spilled from her mouth and she said, "Maybe you won't comeback."

Diamond was perplexed by Reagan's remark "Why would you say something like that?"

"I was hoping that maybe you and Clayton would get re-married on this visit."

Diamond laughed, "We'll see about that."

Reagan arrived at Burton's penthouse at 7 p.m. sharp. She was smartly clad in a butter leather yellow trench coat with complimenting accessories.

Burton asked, "Would you care for a drink?"

"Yes, I'll have a Jack and Ginger neat."

Burton fixed her drink and then sat at the bar while Reagan lounged leisurely on the sofa.

"Burton, I feel so bad for you."

"What do you mean?"

Reagan was hot and she didn't want to waste time. She was the hunter and Burton was the game.

"I'll just come out with it. Diamond is in love with her ex-husband and she has made plans to marry him."

"Did Diamond tell you that?"

"Yes, in a way she did. But she doesn't know how to tell you."

Burton was startled for the moment, feeling the pain that every rejected lover feels but he soon regained his composure.

"Reagan, I don't know why you're here because if what you say is true, this is something for Diamond to discuss with me."

"I'm here as a friend, because I know how lonely you're going to be, when she's out of your life. And I want to be here to help you through it."

Burton asked, "Why are you so concerned and what's in it for you?"

"I don't know what's in it for me but I can show you what's in it for you." Reagan opened her trench coat very slowly and deliberately: flaunting her beautifully sculptured naked body to Burton. Her supple breast stood at full attention, her pubic hair neatly trimmed: as she opened her legs to expose her very receptive vagina. Burton looked shocked and in total disbelief of what had just happened. Once Reagan became aware that Burton was in awe of her, she stood up kicked off her black stiletto pumps, dropped her retro inspired trench-coat coat, and pranced her naked body over towards the bar. Before she was halfway across the room the elevator opened, and Diamond stepped off, and into the living room of Burton's penthouse.

Diamond screamed, "What is this? Reagan what are you doing?"

Burton calmly chimed in, "Yes Reagan why don't you tell her what are you doing, and even better tell why you are here?"

Reagan knew that there could be no logical explanation for her being nude in Burton's apartment so she grabbed her coat and attempted to leave.

Diamond was so furious that she grabbed Reagan by the arm and shoved her down onto the sofa. And in her most demanding voice she said, "You will tell me why you're here."

"I came to tell Burton what you couldn't. You said you didn't want him, so why shouldn't your best friend have him. It stands to reason that when you let him go that someone is going to get him. Why not me? Don't I deserve something good in my life?"

For a moment there was complete silence, and then all of a sudden Reagan started screaming,

"Do you really want to know why I am here? I am here because I am only your shadow. I am here because for all of the years that I've worked for you, I've never gotten the recognition for the projects that I've developed, I've never been anything but your shadow. The station is number one, and you're number one but who am I? I'll tell you who I am. I am your highly paid servant!"

In a very rational low tone Diamond said, "I find you naked in Burtons' apartment and you want to blame me?"

Burton interjected, "Diamond, she came here on the pretense that she needed to talk to me about you. More specifically she said that you didn't know how to tell me that it was over between us."

Diamond could detect the hurt in Burton's voice and she chose not to comment about her breaking up with him.

Reagan said, "Don't worry about firing me because I quit." As Reagan attempted to put on her coat Diamond snatched it from her.

"This is my coat! Or have you forgotten?"

Reagan asked in her most humble voice, "Do you want me to leave naked?"

Diamond with anger in her voice said, "Why not show yourself to the rest of Washington DC? Who knows maybe you'll get lucky!"

Burton made a loud whistle signaling for time out. "Ladies, are you forgetting that I'm news worthy item? I can just see it in tomorrow's **Post**, 'Federal Court of Appeals' Judge involved in Love Triangle' that results in naked woman leaving his condo! I'm not looking to make the front page of tomorrow's paper! Therefore, no one is leaving this apartment naked! Diamond, I want you to let her keep the coat. I'll get you another one."

"Burton, I hope you don't think that I'd ever wear this coat again: not after this female dog had it on!"

Reagan said, "Who are you calling a female dog?"

Diamond said, "I thought I was talking about you but I could be wrong because a dog is loyal to its master. A dog remembers not to bite the hand that feeds him. I guess that makes you lower than a dog."

Reagan answered in a low-spirited voice, "I suppose I am your dog, Mistress Diamond!"

In that instance she picked up her shoes, grabbed Diamond's trench coat and pulled it over her naked body. As she turned to leave, she looked back at Diamond with tears in her eyes and said, "I'm sorry." Diamond turned her back and waited for her to leave.

Once Reagan left, Diamond let out the tears that welled up inside of her. She told Burton that she thought that Reagan was the best friend that she'd ever had. How could she have been so blind? She wondered if it were her fault that the relationship went sour. Burton held her in his arms and assured her that it was not her fault.

"Diamond, if this is the first time in your life that a friend has ever betrayed you, consider yourself lucky."

He told of how he'd lost his best friend in law school because of a girl, and of how he still missed that friendship. Don't make the same mistake. "Maybe you can salvage the relationship?"

"How can I forgive her? And besides you heard her, she really doesn't like me!"

"She likes you but she wants what you have?"

Agreeing with Burton, Diamond said, "If you really listened to her, she wants my life and that's frightening!"

Burton grabbed Diamond around her waist and pulled her body into his, placing her hand on his erect manhood. "This is the one thing that she can't have that belongs to you." He kissed her long and hard until they both felt weak.

After a night of torrid love making, Diamond was so drained, that it stood to reason that she didn't hear Burton as he left for an early morning court session. As she poured a cup of espresso, she thought of how she'd come to tell Burton that it was over but after last night how would she find the strength. She was whipped.

Justin and Erica

Whoever said, "It never rains in southern California" was very much mistaken?

The rain came down, so hard and fast that I thought it would break the glass in my bedroom window. With nothing else to do I was e-mailing back and forth to Shanae Bugatch, as we discussed her wedding plans. Twenty-two year old Shanae was getting married in June to a 27-year-old Yale law school graduate who was serving as a federal prosecutor in Maryland. Personally, I thought he was too old for her but I was still excited for her. I was even more excited that she'd asked me to be in the wedding. It was going to be a June wedding. I couldn't wait to tell Diamond.

My cell phone rang at 11a.m. I recognized the DC area code and I answered without hesitation.

"Hello"

The voice on the other end said, "Its' been a while baby but I was hoping to get with you real soon. Where are you? Are you in D.C.?"

I recognized the voice to be that of Justin Black. He sure had a lot of nerve calling after what he did. I lied "Yes, I'm in DC. What's up Justin?"

"Is that all you got to say to your man after all this time? Damn baby I thought you'd be glad to hear that I beat my charges."

I responded without any enthusiasm in my voice. "Okay Justin, I'm glad for you".

"Yeah baby I made them DC cops look like keystone cops in court." He sounded so arrogant and so full of himself.

I found myself concerned about Sean. "How is Sean?"

"So why are you worried about pretty boy Sean? I ain't hear you ask nothing about how I'm doing. I know you heard he got punked in the bullpen."

"Yes I heard."

"That's just what his punk-ass gets for trying to hang tough when he knows he's soft.

Justin failed to say that he and Sean, his supposedly co-conspirator, was released on a technicality: thanks to Sean's influential family.

I asked, "Is Sean going back to school in DC?"

"Yeah his candy ass is back in school. Look girl, I didn't call you to talk about Sean! What I want to know is when can we hangout? Or are you hung up on

Sean? You better be careful because after what happened to him he might have brought a 'Home in Virginia'.

"What are you saying?"

"You know H.I.V, home in Virginia," he laughed hysterically.

"That isn't funny. I thought he was your friend."

"Erica where is your sense of humor?"

"I don't know. Maybe I left it at Nicky's condo."

"I see that we've got a lot to talk about. Can I see you tonight?"

I asked, "When is the last time that you spoke to Meagan?"

"I haven't seen that bitch since the last time I saw you."

I knew he was lying through his teeth: all 32 pearly whites.

"So now she's a Bitch? I thought you guys were friends."

"I don't know what gave you that idea."

"How is your friend Moe?"

At the mention of Moe's name he became nervous, "Girl, are you crazy? Don't you know better than to mention names on my phone? Let's cut this conversation short and just tell me where to meet you".

I was glad that Justin thought that I was still in DC. I wanted him to go to the restaurant and be as disappointed as I was when I found out he was a liar and a womanizer. All this time I had been comparing him to Carl, when he was nothing but a loser. What could I have possibly seen in him? He was a fake. As far as I was concerned, he didn't even have a soul! Now it was my turn to play with his head. "Okay baby, why don't you meet me at Ole Ted's Bar and Grill around the corner from the Capitol, on 15th Street." I knew the place well, because Diamond and I often frequented it for lunch.

"That sounds real special. Is seven okay?"

"You know, I was hoping to make it later. How about ten o'clock. I was thinking that afterwards we could go to your place."

"Girl don't you be playing with me, because I heard that you are still a virgin."

"Who told you that?"

"Just answer the question. Are you a virgin?"

"Yes, I'm a virgin? Does that mean anything to you?" I knew that it meant nothing to him but I needed to hear him say it.

"Listen up Shortie, I don't want you to get the wrong idea because I'm not trying to get married, and I know you know that I already got one baby. I'm not trying to take care of all of DC."

It was just like I thought: he didn't want anything that resembled a commitment. Who would want a relationship or a baby with this loser?

"Everything is cool. I just wanted you to be my first."

He asked, "Are you sure that you're ready to take this relationship to the next level? Do you know how to protect yourself? Cause I hear that your peeps got money and I don't need them on my back if something happens."

I gave him my most sexy voice, "Something like what? What do you think could happen? Justin, it sounds like you're afraid of me."

"Now why would I be afraid of you, if anything I'm surprised?"

I surprised myself by cracking slick. "I'm surprised that you're backing off. Either you can deliver or you can't. Now show me what you're working with!"

He laughed hysterically, "Girl you sound crazy. You better not get me all hyped up and then back out cause I don't play those kinds of games."

Next he started bragging about the size of his penis: "How do you know that you can take all of this? I'm packing at least eight inches."

I went toe to toe with him. "I'm willing to try, if you can deliver?"

"Girl, I've had women twice your age."

"I can't tell because you sound like you're afraid of me."

Justin went all out to tell me of his sexual prowess. I think he got an orgasm just listening to himself. I got another call while he was in the height of his fantasy. It was Diamond. I made an excuse to Justin and told him that I'd meet him tonight.

I called Justin around 9:30 p.m. and told him that I was unable to meet him because I had an emergency. "Hey Baby, I am sorry but I won't be able to meet you tonight. I have an emergency to deal with."

He was pissed. "You see I knew this shit would happen. You got me all hyped and now your little ass can't come out and play. All you young freaks are the same."

I was enjoying the fact that he was upset and even more that he really wanted me. "Listen baby, I can meet you tomorrow for sure, and this time you can tell me where and when."

"I don't know if I will have time for your little ass tomorrow night. I might be busy. I might be with a real woman."

I called his bluff. "Okay if that's the way that you feel, forget it."

"Hold on girl, I know how much you want me, so I'm going to give you one more chance. If you mess this one up you can forget about me."

I almost burst into laughter. This low-life thought he was flowing.

"Thanks Justin for giving me another chance."

"That's right you better thank your Big Daddy because I know plenty of Bitches that want what I got. Do you feel me? Now listen up. I want you to meet me in the lobby of the downtown Marriott at 8:30 tomorrow night, and you better be wearing something sexy and I don't want no jeans. I want something short and tight. Feel me?"

It was all I could do not to burst into laughter, "Yes Justin, I understand."

"I 'm a grown man, and you are a little girl but when I see you I want you to look like a woman. Feel me? Do you know anything about 69? I'd like for us to get started with that."

"Yeah I like 69." I didn't have a clue as to what he was talking about.

His voice heightened with excitement "Oh, for real? Damn baby, I know that this is going to be banging. I might even take you shopping if you prove to be all that. You like those Prada bags?"

"Oh yes, I love Prada bags." The more I listened to this idiot, the more I disliked him.

14

Dead Men Don't Tell Tales?

Moe had no idea that he was under surveillance as he went about his daily routine of supervising his drug organization. The detectives were waiting to catch him with the goods but he was smart enough to operate his business through the use of pre-paid cell phones and phone cards.

Moses Johnson looked different: he walked different: he felt different, and for the first time in many years he was happy to be alive. He'd even removed his gold teeth and replaced them with pretty white veneers. He was a new man.

He drove back to Capital Street where he'd lived for the past year, and no one seemed to recognize him, mostly because he looked like a million dollar man. Aside from the fact that he'd been working out three or four times a week: he was wearing a three thousand dollar designer suit: his black wavy hair had been cut to precision: and he was driving an S55 Benz.

Lately, when he frequented the clubs and restaurants, the women were giving him mad attention, like he used to get before he was incarcerated. He no longer needed Meagan as his arm candy because he could get any one that he wanted. Moe finally had his game together again.

As he climbed the stairs of his former apartment building to retrieve his mail from the landlord, the familiar stench of cigarettes, urine, and sewage greeted him. He thought, "How he could have lived in a place like this."

He knocked softly on the gray door, with its chipped paint, and graffiti. Ms. Alvarez, Moe's former landlord, had to look twice through the peephole before she recognized Moe. When she realized that it was Moe, she opened the door, hugged him, and told him that she missed him. She remembered that he had been very generous to her. In fact he was probably the best tenant that she'd ever had. Last year he gave her enough money to send for two of her daughters in Puerto Rico. Now it was her turn to help him. She invited him in and informed him that the police had been there several times to inquire about Meagan. She said that she'd been praying for him, and that Meagan seemed like trouble.

"Mr. Johnson, I have been praying for you. Everyday I light a candle for you to be safe. Please know that the white girl is trouble. You must be careful."

Moe collected his mail, thanked her, and gave her a hundred dollar bill for the information …

As he walked out of the building and onto the front steps, he saw a group of heroine junkies hovering around his car. When he tried to get pass them they started asking him for spare change.

One of the guys asked, "Hey brother you got any spare change? I'm just trying to get a sandwich?"

One of the women said that she'd watched his car so that no one would take his wheels, and that she wanted two dollars for looking out for him. "Hey baby I know you got two dollars for me. I been looking out for you and making sure they didn't steal your wheels."

He looked at her in disgust. The woman became even more persistent "Look baby I can give you some serious head for five dollars."

Moe said, "I'm not interested."

"Look man, I know you'll like what I do cause I ain't got no front teeth. The junkie flashed her toothless smile hoping that Moe would be turned on by it. When he continued to ignore her she yelled, "Plus I'm clean. No HIV here!"

It was like she wouldn't take no for an answer.

What really pissed him off was that she had the audacity to touch him. This low-life junkie bitch put her hands on him. Moe had no use or compassion for junkies, so he shoved her down into the street. After this, the others got the message and took off up the street to look for other means to get drugs.

Now he had to decide what to do about Meagan. He should have known that a young college girl from England was bound to have family interested in her whereabouts. He would have to get rid of her because he couldn't risk her talking to the police about his drug operation. What choice did he have? He knew that it wouldn't take much for the police or her family to shake her down after all she was a junkie. He also knew that she would be frightened and weak enough to tell all under pressure and he couldn't take the chance: she had to go.

Alan, Moe and Lobo

Detective Jett sat in front of the apartment building where Meagan and Moe resided. It was almost 12 a.m. and there was still no sign of either Moe or Meagan. It had been a long day for him and he needed some real relaxation. He had about one hour before he was off the clock, so he thought that he'd use the opportunity to pick up one of his hood rats and get his Jimmy waxed before going home to his wife. He was only gone for a few minutes when Meagan and Moe showed up.

Meagan was emaciated to the point that she looked anorexic. She no longer looked like a super model because the drugs had severely affected her appearance. Moe no longer allowed her to walk arm and arm with him. She had to walk behind him just incase he came across something better.

Earlier in the evening Moe called on his henchmen, Alan and Lobo. The three of them sat at Moe's dinning table, systematically making plans to get rid of Meagan. Moe gave the order to OD Meagan and throw her body in a downtown dumpster because those dumpsters were emptied three times a week and there would be a less likely chance of someone discovering her body.

Alan and Lobo arrived at Moe's apartment around 1 a.m. to pick-up Meagan. This was about the same time the surveillance team changed shifts.

Inside of Meagan and Moe's swank apartment, Moe was trying to convince Meagan to make a pick-up with Alan and Lobo. She protested because she was tired but Moe hugged her, and told her he'd wait up for her to return.

"Moe please don't make me go."

"Baby I need you to go with them so that the pickup doesn't look suspicious. You know if the police see a white girl they will be less likely to be suspicious."

She continued to protest. "But I'm tired."

"I promise that I'll wait up for you."

"I'm so sleepy."

"Don't worry you can sleep as long as you like when you get back." He almost laughed as he thought that she was about to go to eternal sleep.

The doorbell rang, alerting Moe that his henchmen were on the scene. Moe kissed Meagan on her forehead and told her it was okay and she left quietly with her executioners.

Once they left the apartment Moe began to have sentimental thoughts about Meagan. He remembered how pretty she was when he first met her. Then he thought about the good lovemaking that had occurred between them. He thought about her oral prowess, as opposed to other women he'd been with. There was no doubt that she enjoyed it. For a fleeting moment he almost called the hit off because he was really going to miss the sex, but what could he do? He couldn't go back to jail.

As Meagan and the two henchmen left the building, the detectives who sat outside, studied Meagan's picture, and then the gaunt presentation of the woman who accompanied the two men. They were only able to recognize her by her red hair and her height. The detectives dimmed the lights on the unmarked car, and followed closely behind the red jeep.

Once they'd gotten the order from Moe, it was Lobo who decided that he would have sex with Meagan before they 'over dosed' her. He fanaticized about when he first met her, and how turned on he was by her accent. What harm would it do and they both could have some fun before she died. Alan on the other hand was a strictly by the book kind of guy and he wanted to follow Moe's instructions explicitly.

Lobo discussed his plan with Alan trying to convince him to join in.

"Look man, you know how I got a thing for that bitch. I was thinking that maybe we could take her to the motel before we knock her off."

"What the hell are you talking about? This is not part of the plan."

"You should think about it man. We could both have a little fun with her."

Alan said, "Man that bitch looks like a swizzle stick, and I ain't trying to take nothing home to my girl."

"I feel you. But man that's a perfectly good piece of ass going to waste."

"Man you know how Moe is. What if something goes wrong?"

"I know what I'm doing. You need to stop trippin about Moe. Did you put the bag of lime in the trunk? Moe said we might need it to hold down the smell."

There was something about Meagan that excited Lobo. He wanted her from the moment he saw her, and when he heard her accent he almost did a melt down. In some ways she reminded him of his man, Pie because both were Caucasian with long slender legs and both wore their hair in a short bob.

Lobo gave Alan a signal, and the jeep came to a halt at a motel off the main strip. By this time Meagan figured out that something was wrong because Moe never mentioned going to a motel. Once they were outside of the car she tried to run. Lobo grabbed her around her waist, and tried to pull her back into the car but he couldn't shut the door because she was kicking and screaming. At this point the officers jumped from their car with guns pointed, and ordered everyone out of the car. The front car door was open. Alan leaned over and pushed Lobo and Meagan from the car, and took off.

Dragging Meagan by the neck, Lobo pulled his gun from beneath his leather jacket, and pointed it to Meagan's head.
"Back off motherf____kers or I will kill this bitch!"
The officer yelled, "Drop the gun and let the girl go."
Lobo held the gun to Meagan's head while he dragged her into the door of the motel lobby screaming,
"I said back the fu__ off". Momentarily he felt a sexual sensation, as he realized that he was finally holding his dream girl. He pulled her even closer to smell her perfume. Little did he know that he would take this last beautiful moment with Meagan, into eternity?

The motel clerk was watching the events unfold like a movie. He was hyped as he reached behind the desk for his gun, and waited for Lobo to enter. When Lobo backed into the lobby, the clerk took aim and fired hitting Lobo in the back. When Lobo dropped, Meagan ran straight into the arms of one of the detectives.

The EMT unit arrived shortly thereafter and said Lobo was critically injured but not dead. He was flown by medi-vac to the nearest shock trauma unit, hanging on to his life, by a thread. Inside the helicopter Lobo's life was flashing before his eyes, as he was being transported to shock-trauma. He could hear one of the officers talking to him but he could hardly respond as he was caught up in the flashbacks of his life. It was like being caught between sleep and reality. His life featured reflections of his past and present

Lobo had not had a real girl friend since he'd gotten out of prison, two years ago. Once in a while after a lap dance, at one of the clubs on the strip, he'd convince a girl to go to a motel with him for a couple hundred dollars. Afterwards, he would return home to his man, Pie. Pie was his lover and companion. Pie was a successful hair stylist, who was beautiful and faithful, and no matter how late it was when Lobo arrived home, he'd find dinner waiting. Pie made sure that Lobo was immaculately groomed from head to toe. His clothes were laid out for him and even his shoes had a spit shine. In fact Pie was the best thing that could have ever happened to Lobo. There was no doubt that Pie was a good wife: at least, he was better than his ex.

Lobo always had a thing for gay men, even before he'd gone to prison, but he'd managed to keep it on the down low: after all, how would he explain it to his boys. He was the most physically fit of his crew. Hell, he'd put in four or five hours a week at the gym. If they ever found out about his relationship with Pie, they would probably label him a bitch, and he couldn't take the chance.

Cassie, his ex-wife, was the only one who knew of his secret life, but who could she tell, after-all she was doing women. They'd both become switch-hitters in foster care while living with old man Bradford and his wife. He'd spent two years in that home, of waking almost every night to old man Bradford going down on him. At first he resisted but after a while he started to enjoy it. He wondered why Mrs. Bradford never suspected anything: that is until he found out that she was getting it on with Cassie. He supposed it didn't matter to her about her husband, as long as her needs were being met.

In 1988, the shit hit the fan when the Bradford's took Jessica in. Jessica Desoto age sixteen was Hispanic and black: a real hottie with a lot of street smarts. At first she went along with the old couples advances. Occasionally, Lobo would awaken in the night to find Jessica sleeping between the old couple. Once Jessica had the Bradford's hooked, she began to extort money from them: threatening to report them to social services if they did not comply. At first it was only two hundred a month but soon she wanted her entire check. The Bradford's had to comply or face jail time. After Lobo and Cassie found out about the money scheme, they also started demanding their checks from the Department of Social Services. It wasn't long before the three juveniles were running the Bradford's household.

One Saturday afternoon, Mr. Bradford, who was approaching his sixty-ninth birthday, drove the three teens into town to the movies. He told them he would pick them up at the mall around 7:30p.m. The three waited all evening for the old man's return. In fact they waited until the mall closed before they decided to catch a cab back to the Bradford's house.

They arrived at home around 11 a.m., only to find the house in total darkness. The Bradfords along with all of their belongings were gone. It was almost as if they'd vanished into the air. The three tried managing the household for a couple months on their own, until the social workers caught up with them and placed them in a group home until their eighteenth birthdays.

Lobo wanted so badly to be given another chance but it was too late. It was getting darker and the flashbacks were becoming dim, and fading. The attendant heard him mumble, "Jesus save me." The curtains closed. His life was over.

When the backup officers arrived, Spank Taggert, the hotel clerk was bragging about how he saved a white girl's life by killing a nigger. He was so caught up in his five minutes of negative fame that he never realized that he'd just been read his rights. The back up officers took him downtown for questioning. On the way to the police station he asked if he should call the local newspaper to let them know how he'd saved a white girl's life. He felt that he should be celebrated as a hero because he did his duty as a patriotic American citizen. He couldn't wait to tell the media that he was born in Pulaski, Tennessee, the birthplace of the Klu Klux Klan, and how he'd met the Grand Wizard in Stone Mountain, Georgia when he was ten years old.

When Spank arrived at the station he was still bragging about his heroic deed. In fact reality didn't hit him until the African American police officer told him that he should call an attorney.

"You got it wrong. Why do I need an attorney?"

"You need an attorney because you shot a man in the back."

"But I saved a white girl's life."

15

Fate and finality

Approximately one hour after the three left, Moe received a call from Meagan's cell phone. He figured his boys were calling to confirm that she was dead, so he answered without reservation.

"Hello."

"Moe I need you to come and get me."

Startled by Meagan's voice, he asked, "Wait a minute. Who is this?"

"Moe baby, it's me Meagan."

He thought he must be dreaming so he sat up in his bed: the same bed that he'd shared with Meagan for the past couple of months.

"Meagan? Where are Alan and Lobo?"

"Lobo got shot at the hotel and Alan took off."

"What are you talking about?" He could not believe what he just heard. He asked her, "Slow your roll and run this by me again?"

Meagan said, "I think that they were trying to rape me because they took me to a motel and you said that we were supposed be going downtown to pick-up something. Any way I tried to run and the cops came. That's when Alan pushed us from the car and drove off. Then Lobo put a gun to my head and the hotel clerk shot him in the back."

Moe thought he was dreaming. How could his plan have been thwarted? "Where are you right now? I mean at this moment?"

"I'm on my way downtown with the police."

He could not believe what he was hearing, "Did you say that you are with the police?"

"Yeah, I am in the back seat of a patrol car."

"What the hell are you doing with the police?"

"They told me that my Uncle Sydney and his boss Diamond are looking for me, and they want me to tell them about Lobo and Alan."

"Did they ask about me?" He was nervous as he asked her again with firmness in his voice, "Did you tell them anything about me?"

"No why would I?"

"Listen up girl, whatever you do, don't tell them anything, especially about me. Do you understand me?"

"Moe I love you. I would never let you down."

"I don't want to hear that! And why the fu_k are you mentioning my name?"

"But Moe, you know that I need you."

"You stupid bitch, didn't I tell you not to mention my name?" He didn't wait for her answer. He slammed the phone down, and with his head in his hands he screamed aloud, "This junkie bitch is going to send me back to prison."

He paged Alan with a 911 code. Reluctantly, Alan answered, "Yeah Moe, I was just about to call you."

"Man, just tell me how you and Lobo fucked this thing up. Did you know that the cops got Meagan and it's no telling what she told them?"

"Moe don't blame me for this."

"Who should I blame? Tell me who is responsible for the fu_k-up?"

"Man you know that Lobo is sex crazy. He can't turn anything down. He thought it wouldn't matter if he did her, since we was going to off her anyway."

"So what you are telling me is that all this was Lobo's idea? And you ain't have shit to do with nothing?"

"You got to believe that it was all Lobo's idea."

"I heard you punked out and pushed them out of the car."

"You tell me, what choice did I have?"

"Did you know that Lobo was shot and by now he maybe dead? If he's still alive he may talk, and if he does talk, I don't want either of us implicated."

"What do you want me to do?"

"I want you to pick up Sweetman, and switch the plates on your car. Then I want you to drive to your cousin's in South Beach, and lay low until you hear from me."

"You want me to go to Florida? What about my girl and my baby?"

"What about them? You made the choice not to follow orders. Now you've got consequences. You are damn lucky that I believe your story. So the last thing that you want to do is piss me off. Where is your stash?"

"Everything that I got is at my girl's house."

"I want you to go there right now. Tell her that something happened, and that you need to lay low for a while. Don't tell her where you are going. Just get your shit and get out fast! And whenever you call her from now on, I want you to block the number, or use a calling card. Do you understand me?"

"Okay Moe whatever you say."

"Man your ass is lucky! Now don't let me catch your ass back in DC, until I tell you that it's safe."

"I'm going to call Sweetman, and tell him to meet you at the joint in one hour. Make sure that you are there with everything."

Alan knew the deal, and even better, he knew Moe. He would pick up his money: meet Sweetman and he would be killed. The two hundred fifty grand that he had on him would be split between Moe and his killer. He had to move fast, and he had to take his girl and his baby with him otherwise he might not ever see them again.

Tricia was asleep when Alan called, and she could hardly understand what he was saying. He told her to grab a few things for herself and the baby. He said she should leave out of the house right now. She should park her car on the next street, and he would meet her in fifteen minutes.

"You need to tell me what's going on?

"I don't have time to explain."

"If you can't explain, I'm not leaving."

"Don't make this difficult. You only got about fifteen minutes total time to get your things and the baby's things together."

"I'm not going anywhere with my baby in the middle of the night."

"Listen up girl, because this is the only thing that I am going to explain to you. Moe has a contract on me. If I leave town and leave you behind, he is going to kill you and the baby. Do you feel me?"

"What about my house and my job? When can we come back?"

"I'll get someone to take care of the house. I don't know when we can come back."

Tricia thought for a moment, about everything that had transpired between the two of them. She'd met Alan three years ago while working the midnight shift at the hospital. He'd come in as a gunshot wound victim in to the Emergency Room of the hospital where she worked. She'd seen him through his three-week stay at the hospital. They started dating as soon as he was released from the hospital. At first it was on the pretense that he needed someone to check his wound on a daily basis but after a few visits to his 'player' apartment coupled with the good sex, she was hooked.

Alan was good-looking with a beautiful head of long brown locks, and he had lots of money to spend. At age 35, Tricia was 10 years Alan's senior but with her youthful appearance no one who saw them together gave it a thought. Two years later she became pregnant with his baby. They had not planned for baby Ian but after his arrival they couldn't imagine life without him. Last year Alan gave her the down payment on a new home in Rockville. It was a beautiful home that sat on an acre lot, and it had every convenience that she could think of. When her parents questioned her about Alan's source of income she told them that Alan was in real estate. Although, she knew the kind of business he was in, she never thought that it would in any way affect her life. Now she would be on the run like a fugitive.

Tricia had been a nurse at St Matthews for ten years and for the past three, she was the Emergency Room charge nurse. As she grabbed her nurses' license and her college degree off the wall, and placed them at the bottom of the baby's bag, she wondered how to explain her sudden move to her parents and to her employer. But there was no time for reflection or regrets. She dumped her clothes and the baby's clothes into several garbage bags, and put them into the trunk of her car. When the baby was safely placed in his car seat, she backed her 735 Beamer out of the garage, and drove down the street onto Charter Grove, where she turned off the lights and waited for Alan.

It was 4 am when Alan pulled up into the driveway. He was careful to make sure that no one was following him. He went inside the house and downstairs to the basement where he kept his safe. He emptied its contents into a duffle bag, walked back up stairs, and turned every light on in the house to make it look as if he were there. When he finished gathering a few personal items, he threw the duffle bag over his shoulder, and left out the back door. He crossed over two lawns and climbed a privacy fence, to get to the next street, where Tricia and the baby were waiting for him.

Alan knew that Moe would expect him to retreat to Miami, so he decided to go to New York. Moe would never find him in Manhattan and he had close friends there. The plan was that they would stay in a hotel for the first week, and then they would look for an apartment in Queens. After a month or two Tricia could begin working again, and Alan could look for a legitimate job. Maybe in time he would renew his teaching certificate or start a home improvement business. After all, he was the only one of the crew who didn't have a criminal record, making it easy for him to blend into the mainstream again. At any rate he was done with Moe and the drug scene.

Moe had already begun to fanaticize about life with Tricia. Tricia was tall and well built with big legs, and Moe would do just about anything for a big-leg girl. She was medium brown, with golden brown, shoulder length hair. She was a professional woman, and most importantly she didn't use drugs. She would be a welcomed change from Meagan. Tricia was the kind of woman he dreamed about while in prison. He thought he would start out by bringing her nice gifts for the baby, and then work his way up to buying presents for her. In no time at all she would be his woman, maybe even before Christmas. He couldn't wait for his mother to meet her because he was tired of hearing his mother say that he hadn't had a decent woman since his wife.

Around 5am Moe called Sweetman to find out if things had gone as planned. He was hoping that Alan was dead, and that he would get a chance with his fine stallion of a woman.

"What's the word?"

"Man no happenings here."

"What do you mean? Didn't he show up?"

"Naw man, it's like I said no happenings."

"Do you mean he was a no show?"

"He didn't call to say that he wasn't coming, so I waited here like you told me."

"Man I don't believe this! Pick me up in front of my place in thirty minutes. We're going to pay Alan a surprise visit. I've got a feeling that he's at home with his girl trying to get that last little bit."

When Moe and Sweetman arrived, Alan's car was in the driveway and it appeared that every light in the house was on. They parked on the opposite side of the street, and waited for Alan to come out. As the sun began to come up Moe decided to call Alan. When he didn't get an answer he decided to knock on the door. Sweetman ran around to the back of the house to try to enter through the sliding glass door but when he tampered with the lock, the alarm went off causing both men to retreat to the car. Moe told Sweetman to park further down the street so that they could watch to see if Alan would leave his house.

Just as they reached the sign that said New York/95 north, the alarm service called Tricia on her cell phone to let her know that the alarm at her house was sounding off.

"Hello."

"Miss West?"

"Yes this is Miss West."

"This is your alarm service calling to inform you that your alarm is going off."

Tricia answered very professionally, "Can you send someone to my house to check on it because I am on my way out of town?"

"Yes we will alert the police. If there is a problem may we call you back at this number?"

"Yes, and thank you very much."

Alan assured her that everything would be fine and that in a couple of days he would call his sister to check on things at the house.

They arrived in New York around 9:30 in the morning. After parking the car in a garage in SoHo, Tricia and Alan took a cab to Herald Square, where they checked into a hotel. After showering and changing they took to the streets to shop for clothes and necessities for the baby.

In a month or so they would sell the house and break clean of Moe and the underworld. Moe told Sweetman that he had a gut feeling that Alan skipped town. He said it was just as well, at least now he wouldn't be available to talk, or testify to anything. Now that Alan was out of the way, he needed to shut Lobo down.

16

The Reality of it All

Diamond's phone rang about 3 a.m. while she was in a deep sleep. It was the police calling her to say that they'd found Meagan, and to ask what they should do with her.

"Ms. Redfren sorry to call you at this hour but the commissioner said we should call you as soon as we found the girl."

Diamond, awakened from a deep sleep tried to collect her thoughts as best she could, answering, "Yes that is correct. Where is she?"

"Our men picked her up tonight. She's in pretty bad shape. We hardly recognized her from the picture that you gave us. May I recommend drug rehabilitation for her?"

Momentarily she thought about her precious granddaughter Erica and how she'd allowed her to go out with Meagan. Why had she been so lenient? She had been much more careful with Miles. The guilt was overwhelming. What if this had happened to Erica? She would never have forgiven herself.

"Give me a half hour, and I'll be there."

She was so sleepy that she could hardly see the numbers on the phone as she dialed Sidney to tell him the news.

Sydney arrived at Diamond's house in twenty minutes. Diamond tried very tactfully to prepare him for the worst "The main thing Syd is that she's alive, and where there is life there is hope."

Sidney hysterically said, "Diamond, please don't beat around the bush with me."

"Okay, I'll be frank. The detectives said she's in bad shape and that she needs drug rehabilitation."

"Oh my God what will I tell her mother?"

"Tell her we found her and that's she's safe."

"This is my fault. I should have monitored her activities more closely. Maybe if I'd spent more time with her? I promised her mother, that I would take good care of her, but I failed."

"Sydney what happed to Meagan isn't your fault. You can't blame yourself. What we need to do is work together to get her back on track."

When they arrived at the police station they were led into a room where Meagan sat teary eyed. When Sydney approached her, she hung her head in shame. He grabbed her and held her like she was a baby. He said he didn't want to question her right now: there would be time for that later. Diamond on the other hand, stepped out of the interrogation room to begin the process of calling for a rehab placement for Meagan.

One of the detectives questioned Meagan to find out about how much she knew about her attackers. She told the police that they were two guys that she'd met at a party a few weeks ago.

"When you got into the car with the two men on Georgia Avenue, it appeared as if you knew them."

Meagan said, "Their names are Alan and Lobo. They are friends, of a friend of mine."

"What is your friends' name?"

Sydney interjected, "Is she being charged with something? Does my niece need a lawyer?"

"No she doesn't need a lawyer at this time, and no she is not being charged. We just need to question her about her involvement with a man named Moses Johnson, and the other two men that we found her with. If it is okay with you sir, I would like to continue." Sydney nodded giving his approval.

Detective Contee decided he would pick-up where the other left off, playing good cop, and bad cop.

"How are we doing Meagan? Can I get you anything? Maybe you'd like a soda, perhaps a cup of coffee, or some water?"

"No thanks." What she needed, he did not have. What she needed was a hit because she was feeling on edge.

The detective turning to Sydney asked, "How about you sir, what can I get for you?"

"I'll take a cup of coffee. Make it strong and black."

The other detective left to get a cup of coffee for Sydney, while Detective Contee continued to question Meagan. "Meagan I hear that you are well acquainted with a Mr. Moses Johnson."

Meagan was scared out of her mind from just hearing the cops mention Moe's name. She didn't know how to answer the detective, and she knew that she had to be careful not to mention Moe's name. "I don't know a Moses Johnson."

"My sources tell me differently. Am I correct in assuming that you have been living with him for the past couple of months at a condo on 'Capital Hill'?

Meagan glanced at Sydney, and in a very infantile voice she said, "Uncle Sydney, I'd like to go home now."

Sydney looked straight in to his nieces' eyes and said, "Meagan I want you to tell them all about this Moses Johnson. It is obvious that he is not a very nice person."

"That's putting it lightly", Officer Contee chimed in "This man has served 25 years in Federal prison on Kingpin charges and serving that kind of time in prison does something to a man's psychic. Our gut feeling is that he was tipped off that we were looking for you, and that he put a hit out on you to keep you from talking about his operation."

She was stunned as she said, "What do you mean a hit?"

"We mean that he was trying to have you killed. The guy whom you know as Lobo is Bernard Branch. He served six years in Lorton for conspiracy to commit murder."

Meagan thought for a moment: Moe a kingpin and Lobo an attempted murderer, this was more than she could fathom. It was more than strange that Moe insisted that she go out with Lobo and Alan tonight because he'd never asked her to do anything like that before. What if he was trying to get rid of her? After all he'd been treating her bad for the last couple of weeks, telling her that she looked like death on a stick. No, she refused to believe that the man who'd made love to her this morning would try to have her killed tonight. These cops were playing with her mind because the Moe she knew would never harm her.

Detective Carrusi walked in with two cups of coffee in badly stained cups with the news that Lobo was dead. In a very calm and overly dramatic voice, Detective Carrusi said, "Your friend Lobo is dead. But before Lobo died, he confessed in the presence of police officers, that Moe asked him to kill you." He leaned over and put his face in Meagan's' face with his voice heightened for effect, as he repeated, "He was supposed to kill you!"

The two detectives left the room to talk in the hall for a moment. When they returned they took turns questioning Meagan about Alan and Lobo. Meagan stuck to her story that they were friends that she'd met at a party. As the informal interrogation continued, Meagan started fidgeting and scratching: a sure sign that she was addicted.

"Look I told you that I don't know any Moe."

"Why are you trying to protect a man who is trying to kill you? We know that you cohabitated with him for at least two months. This man is being investigated by the Feds, and if you continue to lie you will face jail time."

Meagan started to feel confused. Her brains were scrambled from the drug use. She was totally lost without Moe to tell her what to do."

Detective Carrusi told Sydney that Meagan was going to need a lawyer because they could not accept her story about not knowing Moe Johnson. They also informed her that the Feds would probably want to question her. "If she lies to the Feds she will face serious jail time." Sydney begged Meagan saying, "Please tell them the truth, and everything that you know." Meagan wished she could explain to her uncle that going to jail would be a piece of cake compared to facing Moe's wrath.

Without warning Meagan stood up and thanked everyone for his or her help and attempted to leave. Just as she rose from her chair, Diamond walked into the interrogation room and said that she'd found a place for Meagan, at the Tree Light Rehab Center in Westminster, Maryland. Meagan said, "I am not going to rehab. Why do I need rehab?"

As she tried to leave Detective Brogden blocked her path. "It seems as if everyone wants to help you, but you don't see the need to help yourself. Now I'm offering you two choices, either you go to rehab or we lock you up on the charge of withholding pertinent information regarding a felony, and failure to cooperate."

"I thought that you weren't going to arrest me?"

Diamond intervened, "Meagan you're not thinking clearly, we only want to help you to get better."

Meagan became outraged at what she thought was Diamond's patronizing approach.

Meagan screamed on Diamond, "Diamond you maybe able to tell my uncle what to do, but I don't work for you! And you aren't my mother! So leave me the hell alone!"

Diamond whispered to the officers that she was going to need some assistance.

Meagan overheard Diamond, grabbed her purse and asked to go to the ladies room. Her intent was to exit through a side door. One of the detectives tried to take her purse from her. As he grabbed the purse the contents spilled out on to the table. Among the items in the purse were a make-up bag, a cell phone and two vials of a white substance.

Detective Brogden took one of the vials, tasted its content and labeled it as heroine. Detective Contee read Meagan her rights and she was taken into custody.

Sydney with tears streaming down his face said, "What do I need to do to get her released?"

Detective Brogden answered, "She will have to be held over until the Court Commissioner arrives.

If she doesn't have any priors, more than likely she'll be released on her own reconnaissance."

Diamond slipped out into the hall and made a call to the police commissioner on his private line.

"Good morning Kurt. This is Diamond. I need a favor."

It was 6 am. And Kurt half asleep answered, "You got it baby."

"Your men found the girl that I was looking for but unfortunately she had two vials of heroine in her purse, and they've taken her into custody. What can I do to help her get released?"

"Diamond, I'm afraid she's more involved than you think. The man that she's been living with is being investigated by the FBI as we speak."

"Are we talking about this Moe Johnson character?"

"Yes, the notorious King-pin Moses Johnson. Even if we release her, she'll probably run right back to him. And if that happens, her life won't be worth anything. Trust me on this. He will kill her to keep her from talking to the Feds."

"Let me be the first to inform you that he made an attempt on her life tonight. Two men who work for him tried to kill her, but luckily your men were on the scene before it went down. To make a long story brief, one of men confessed before he died, that Moses Johnson asked him to kill Meagan."

"I need to get dressed and get down to headquarters. If all of this information rings true, I will issue a warrant for Mr. Johnson before the Feds get here. By the way your girl is going to need to go into one of our safe houses."

Diamond was silent for a moment while she envisioned her beautiful innocent granddaughter in the company of this Moe person. She wanted to kiss and slap Erica all at the same time.

Kurt asked, "Diamond, are you listening?"

"Yes Kurt, I hear you. What if we put Meagan in rehab until you need to talk to her?"

"No. Not a good idea. What is to prevent her from walking away from rehab?"

"Listen because I know what I'm doing. I've already made arrangements for her to enter one of those lock-down facilities in Western Maryland. I was told escape without help is impossible at this facility, and that means that Moe won't have access to her either."

"If you're that sure, I'll have two of my men escort her right now but I'd better check it out just to be sure."

"Kurt, I owe you."

"You don't owe me anything. As always, I'm happy to help a pretty lady in distress, and besides if we hadn't been looking for your girl, we would never have found out that Moses Johnson was still in business."

"Thanks Kurt. I'll call you soon."

If only she were sincere about calling him, he'd be the happiest man in the world. He knew that the only time that she would be calling was if she needed a favor and maybe to wish him happy holiday.

He glanced to the other side of the bed where Heather was lying with wide-opened eyes, in her jeweled V-string with black satin trim, listening to his conversation. He wanted her dressed and out of his place, and he hoped that she wouldn't say anything to make him mad because she was only a fill in until the real thing came along: or until Diamond came to her senses about their relationship.

Heather in a demanding tone asked Kurt, "So Kurt what does the 'Queen of Everything' need this time?" Heather hated Diamond personally and professionally. She'd been a temp in her office for six months until the lead secretary gave her the boot. She'd asked to speak with Diamond personally but Diamond was too busy and referred her to Reagan. Reagan simply said, "Didn't you read your contract? You were hired as a temp and that gives us the option to either extend your six-month contract or terminate it. Now is there anything else that I can help you with?" Heather answered, "No" and left.

Heather and Kurt met in therapy. She was dealing with a recent divorce, and he the break-up with Diamond. He blamed himself for the break-up with Diamond, rationalizing that if he'd asked her to marry him, they might be still together.

Twenty-eight year old, Swedish-born Heather, very seductively let down her blond hair on to her black lace top. She was vision loveliness as she gave Kurt her most seductive pose, only to hear him say in a nonchalant voice, "Get dressed! I need to get down to the station ASAP."

Disappointed and hurt, Heather screamed, with the blue veins bulging in her neck, "I'm tired of your obsession with Diamond. This is positively the last time that I am coming over here. You can just forget about me!"

Kurt walked quickly into the bathroom and locked door but not before digging the knife a little deeper. With a laughter in his voice he said, "Okay Heather, consider yourself an after thought!"

Heather picked up a glass from the Bombay chest beside the bed and threw it at the door, shattering the glass into little pieces.

Diamond had been Kurt's girl for four years. At the time of their courtship he was Police commissioner of the DC police department. Kurt was flamboyant: a real clothes horse. In fact he probably had just as many clothes in his closet as did Diamond. Kurt was known around town as a lady's man. When he walked into a room everyone took notice, especially the ladies. The relationship worked for Diamond because she never wanted a commitment from him, and besides that, she loved hearing about the police work in DC. The relationship was light-hearted and fun, until the night that Kurt stopped by her house without calling.

The two had plans to attend the Mayor's inaugural ball but Diamond had to beg-off at the last minute, because her son was coming to town. She never bothered to explain to Kurt, as to why she had to cancel. He assumed she had plans to spend her evening with someone else.

It was around mid-night when Miles and Diamond arrived home from a late dinner at Diamond's sister's home on the Potomac River. They could not have been in the house for more than ten minutes when the doorbell rang. It was Kurt, and he was loaded. With five shots of Remy XO in his system, he was loud and obnoxious, accusing Diamond of an affair with the younger man who answered the door.

Reeking with the smell of alcohol, Kurt asked Miles, "What the hell are you doing here? Where's Diamond?"

Miles seemed to think Kurt's behavior was amusing until he pulled his jacket back to reveal his gun.

"Hold on Brother. This is my mother's house."

Kurt knew that she had a son but he wasn't expecting a man in his thirties.

Kurt, nearly shocked into sobriety said, "Your mother?"

"Yes sir, Diamond is my mother! And may I ask who are you and why are you brandishing your firearm?"

Maintaining her composure to avoid conflict, Diamond interjected, "Miles darling this is Kurt Stancil, a good friend of mine. Kurt is the Police Commissioner for the District of Columbia. Kurt this is my son, Miles Redfern."

Kurt looked dumbfounded. Breaking the ice, Miles asked Kurt if he'd like to come in for coffee. "You look as if you could use a strong cup of coffee."

"No thank you, I think I'll be heading home." He was embarrassed that he'd made a fool of himself especially in the presence of Diamond. "Nice meeting you son." He stumbled out of the door in a drunken stupor, and into his car where his driver waited.

"Mom I hate to get in your business but this man appears dangerous. Suppose you'd had a gentleman caller, rather than me?"

"You are absolutely correct. It could've gotten ugly. I'll speak with Kurt in the morning."

"Don't just speak to him. Get rid of him!"

"Thank you for your concern. But I'll handle this in my own way."

"Just be careful."

Diamond thought, some things are blessings in disguise. She'd wanted to end the affair months ago because this was not the first time that Kurt had acted in a brash manner. This was the perfect out for her. Besides she'd met a handsome judge at a silent auction fundraiser and he'd already called her twice. With Kurt out of the picture, she would be free to date the Judge.

17

Rainbow Seeker

Diamond walked in to find Reagan clearing out her office. With a grimacing facial expression Reagan said,

"I'll be out of you way shortly."

"And where do you think you are going?"

"I am not sure but far away from here."

"Did you forget that you are under contract?

"I am fully aware that I am under contract!"

"You will forfeit everything if you quit. Are you sure that you want to do that? And besides where am I going to find someone to replace you?"

"Do you mean that that you would actually hold me to contract after what transpired at Burton's?

Diamond in a stern voice answered, "You're damn right I would!"

"But why do you want me to stay? You know that it will never be the same between us again."

"Reagan, I thought I taught you better than that. Why are you trying to mix our business relationship with our personal one? How I feel about you personally, has nothing to do with our business relationship. You are good at what you do for the station, and that's what's important to me. So unless you want to walk out of here with nothing but a letter of reference, you need to start unpacking. And check your calendar because we have two very important meetings this afternoon."

Before Reagan had time to digest what had just happened, Diamond disappeared down the hall and into her own office. Reagan took a deep breath as a sigh of relief. She knew in her heart of hearts that Diamond would not have any trouble finding a replacement for her. So why was she holding on to her? Never in her life had she met anyone like Diamond. In her hood, back in Harlem, messing with your main girl's man was grounds for getting your ass-kicked, if not worse. She wondered if they could ever be friends again.

After work she decided to celebrate the fact that she still had a job. She took a drive over to a Jazz Club in Tacoma Park.

Reagan was a vision of beauty in her vintage knee-length brown cashmere coat and tan wool embroidered necklace on a dress, as she walked into the club, sat down on the bar and ordered a glass of 'California Blush'. Halfway through her drink, a tall well-dressed man asked if the seat beside her was taken. Reagan checked him out from head to toe before answering, "No."

He was a very handsome and distinguished looking gentleman, and she could definitely use the company.

"Looks like you've had a hard day. Can I get you another drink?" From her response he would be able to tell if she was as classy as she looked. From experience he knew that a street girl would have quickly ordered another drink whether she was finished the one in front of her or not: and one that was more expensive than the one that she was drinking. It was the nature of the hood-rat to try to get over.

"No thanks. I'm still nursing this one."

He asked, "Do you come here often?"

Reagan turned around and looking into his eyes she said, "Only when I need to relax."

"I hope that I'm not disturbing you."

"You're fine." And she meant that in several ways, not only was he good looking but he was sexy, as well.

The two struck up a great conversation and discovered that they had a lot in common. He was delightfully charming and appeared to be well read. In her mind he was what you'd call a smooth operator.

After a few drinks they decided to go back up town to dinner.

He called ahead to make reservations at an exclusive restaurant in Bethesda.

They walked into the restaurant holding hands and looking into each other's eyes as if they were already lovers.

The waiter asked him if he'd like a wine list. Hardly glancing at the list, he asked the waiter to bring him a bottle of his best house wine. The waiter, doubting his ability to pay a thousand dollars for the bottle of wine, quoted the price before serving him. "The best house wine is one thousand dollars a bottle. Perhaps Sir would like to be served wine by the glass rather than the bottle."

That really pissed him off but he couldn't afford to get off in the presence of his new lady, so he decided to go the professional route, and play the race card. "I'd like to see the manager?" A small middle-eastern man appeared and identified himself as the restaurant manager. He explained that the waiter had insulted him as he questioned his ability to pay for the wine, and he felt that it was based on his race. The manager quickly resolved the situation by giving him the bottle of wine, compliments of the house, along with the promise that this would be the waiter's last evening at the restaurant.

Both Reagan and her new friend became so deeply engaged in conversation that they hardly touched their meal of escargots, veal kidney, and goat cheese over garden greens.

By 10 p.m., he'd talked her into going to his place for nightcap. Reagan thought, "What the hell? He had the right look; the right car; and a seemingly endless cash flow", so she thought she'd take a chance. She left her car in a downtown parking lot and rode with her new friend. Once inside the car he leaned over and slid his hand down the base of her neck. His very touch excited her beyond belief, and she found herself powerless to his touch.

When they arrived at his apartment he poured two glasses of Dom into crystal flutes, as he began his subtle ritual of seduction. They talked, they danced, they laughed and they drank until she passed out. Around 3:30 am, he lifted her from the sofa and tucked her into his bed, while he slept in the den.

The next morning Reagan awakened to the smell of fresh coffee. With her eyes wide open she checked out the apartment that she'd been unable to see in her drunkenness of last evening. There were furnishing by 'Roche Bobois and Henredon'. The man was living large but she'd have forgotten his name except for the large signature painting behind the bed, Moses Johnson. She wondered if he were an artist by profession.

When he realized that she'd awakened, he brought in a tray of scrambled eggs, fresh croissants, strawberries and mimosa. Her face was still luminous, and her beautiful brown shoulder length hair was hardly out of place. He wondered about her age: guessing it was somewhere between twenty-nine and thirty-nine, as he thought how beautiful she looked in the early morning.

After breakfast, he filled the Jacuzzi with luxurious bath salts and bubble bath: and very humbly asked if she would allow him to bathe her.

"Would you do me the honor of allowing me to bathe you?"

Reagan's mother had always warned her, that anything or anyone that seemed too good to be true probably was. She told her mother, whom she now considered to be her conscious, since her death two years ago, to but out. She heard herself answer him ever so softly "That would be nice."

Moe took her by the hand and led her in to the bathroom where sweet exotic perfumed scents permeated her nostrils. Reagan sat down in the warm Jacuzzi while Moe leaned over the Jacuzzi and lathered her ever so gently. When he felt she could no longer resist him, he asked her if it was okay to touch her down there. There was something about the way he asked to touch her that made her feel like a teenage girl who was about to lose her virginity. Rather than answer him, she spread her legs, so that he could begin the delicate washing, and deliberate rubbing of her Clit.

After she reached an orgasm, Moe helped her to stand to her feet and began drying her voluptuous body. The next thing that she felt was the rhythmic motion of Moe's tongue sweeping in and out of her vagina, sort of like the best vibrator that she'd ever owned. With one leg in the bath and the other on the top of the tub, he clasped his mouth tightly over her vagina, so that none of her escaped him: Moe brought her to orgasm. The orgasm was so intense that she nearly fell backwards into the tub. When he was finished he rinsed her body once more before towel drying her.

With Barry White bellowing out the lyrics of "Secret Garden" in the background, neither spoke as Reagan lie on the bed and waited for Moe to put on a condom. Moe could tell that this girl loved sex, and that his performance at this very moment would either make or break the relationship between the two of them. Moe was no amateur to the game of love. He'd thought ahead, taking Viagra before show time to ensure optimum performance.

Moe was colossal and he took her to a place where no other had. He was so deep in her that she felt she was going to faint. Not to be out done, when it was her turn on top: she put her heart and soul into it, but she was no match for Moe and Viagra. And so it was she, who signaled timeout.

One hour later Reagan called her job to say that she'd be unavailable today and that all appointments should be cancelled and calls should be directed to her secretary.

18

Rehab

Meagan rinsed her face twice before beginning her daily make-up ritual.

Today she would meet with her attorney, the federal prosecutor, and a Federal Agent. Today was the day that she would bring Moe and his entire operation down. She still found it unbelievable that her ex-lover Moe Johnson tried to have her killed and now he would pay for not having completed the job. In return for her informing on Moe, the Feds promised she would receive a half-million dollars and a full scholarship to Oxford University in England.

As she glanced into the badly streaked mirror, she recognized herself, for the first time in months. Her complexion was clear: her checks rosy and she'd gained about twelve pounds. She was very careful when she put on her make-up because Diamond warned her to avoid a dramatic look because of the nature of the investigation. She must appear to be the victim and not a participant in Moe's drug operation.

Yesterday, Uncle Sydney and Diamond came to visit her. Diamond brought her a stunning green beaded cardigan sweater, with a drop waist black tweed midcalf skirt to wear for the interview. She looked like the 1950s essence of innocence.

She'd been in rehab for six weeks and she was looking better and feeling stronger than she'd felt in months. There was one thing that she learned in last night's group session that stood out from the other mundane jargon, and that was most recovering addicts are horney as hell. The group leader said in most cases drugs and alcohol were suppressants of the addict's sexual appetite: and once the addict's system was purged of drugs, they would be screwing like rabbits. She even passed out condoms as if they expected the residents to screw each other.

The rehab was crazy: mostly rich kids with drug problems, wearing lots of pricey clothes and expensive jewelry. Where did Diamond find this place? It was much better than the apartment that she shared with her uncle and even better, the food was superb. Shrimp salad and crab balls were on last night's menu. This place was bordering country club status.

On her first day she met Beth a twenty-one-year old heiress to the Crown Corporation who had been in and out of this place since she was thirteen. Beth had been using since she was ten years old. With her pink and black hair, and her twenty-one body piercings, she looked like a cross between a Goth, and a drag queen.

Loquacious Beth was more than happy to give Meagan the 411 on the rehab. She said the program was divided into four levels. She told her that if she wanted to progress to level four she should be real nice to Dr. Garfield because his report counted more than the counselors. Beth put her down with Doctor Garfield's game. She told her to go into the first session pretending to be completely help-less and to be sure to hug him at the end of the session, making sure that she pressed her leg into his as she hugged him. This would signal him that she was in agreement with his terms. At the next session she should wear a skirt or dress, with no panties, and sit so that the good doctor would be able to look under her dress.

Dr. Garfield the rehab psychologist was a forty-year old nerd. He was tall and thin, with thick horn rimmed glasses, and a gait walk. His office, like his clothing smelled of mothballs and tobacco. He spent most of his time at the rehab, rather than going home to his cluttered efficiency apartment in Northwest DC.

The first session went as Beth said it would. Meagan pretended to hang onto the doctor's every word while all the time she was laughing in her heart. He wanted to know why she started using drugs. Did she have a bad childhood? Which one of her parents molested her? How often did she masturbate? Meagan could not believe that rich intelligent people were paying top dollars to have their kids listen to this kind of bullshit. She wanted to tell him that she'd started using drugs to help her stay awake to keep up with her studies while working a full-time job. There was no other reason. But that was not what this ass-hole wanted to hear. At the end of the first session, she walked into the doctor's arms and pressed her leg between his. She held him very tightly until she felt a bulge in his pants. He grabbed her buttocks and squeezed it tightly before letting her go.

A week later, Meagan strolled into her second session dressed in a white tee shirt and a short blue denim skirt. When she became bored with his questions, and the smell of his office, that seemed to pervade her olfactory senses: she opened her legs and exposed her vagina to him. Dr. Garfield continued talk for a minute or two before kneeling down between her legs. When it was over he got up wiped his mouth with a dingy white handkerchief and concluded the session as if nothing sexual had occurred. Meagan was insatiable, and it didn't matter that the Doc was less than desirable, besides she didn't have to accommodate him and she needed to get off. It had been at least six weeks since she'd engaged in sex with Moe and she was desperate. When it was over she tried to talk to the Doc about what had just occurred but he acted as if it never happened.

"Doc did you know that you give pretty good head. When can we get together again?"

"Your next appointment is one week from today."

"Suppose I need to get with you before that time."

"I am afraid that would be impossible because my schedule won't permit. In fact, I am booked solid for the rest of the week."

"So you give head, by appointment only?"

Doctor Garfield looked at Meagan with utter disdain.

"Meagan, I am afraid that I am going to have to ask you to leave because I have another client coming in."

Meagan opened the door and left but not before whispering to the young man walking in, "He gives good head." The doctor never blushed and very dogmatically asked the next client into his office.

The first person to arrive on the scene was the federal prosecutor. She watched from the window of the reception area as the handsome young-man walked up the path to the front door of the rehab center. When the attendant presented him in the reception area, he introduced him to her as the federal prosecutor.

He had an infectious smile, and Meagan found herself easily smiling back at him. He was handsome with a warm persona, sort of like a modern day prince charming. And she immediately began fanaticizing about him. "I wonder what it would be like to make love to such a man." Strangely enough he bore an uncanny resemblance to Moe. Her fantasy was interrupted as the federal prosecutor extended his hand for a handshake.

"You must be Meagan?"

"Yes."

"It is good to meet you Meagan. My name is Jason Johnson."

"It is good to meet you as well."

She looked into his eyes and wondered why she'd been unable to meet a man like him. Most of the guys that she'd met since she arrived in America were drug dealers or nerds. She was beginning to believe that guys like this one only existed in the movies.

"Would you like to get started or would you rather wait for your attorney?"

She thought, "You'd better believe that I like to get started." What she meant is that she'd like to start a real relationship with him. She was thinking about something old fashioned like candy, flowers, walks in the park and maybe even kids.

"Yes, I'd like to get started."

He smiled, and pulled out his tape recorder.

"Would you please state your name, address, and birth date for the record?"

Before Meagan had the chance to respond, her attorney Warren Powers walked in and the conversation came to a halt.

"Meagan I hope that you weren't coerced into making a statement before I arrived."

"No sir we were just chatting about the weather."

"Good. We'll get started as soon as Agent Clark arrives."

Agent Reggie Clark was the last to arrive. He arrived forty-five minutes late with his contract and recorder in hand.

The session ended in less than an hour.

To Meagan's surprise Agent Clark announced that Meagan would be required to meet with the Mr. Johnson the federal prosecutor as well as himself at the federal courthouse on the following Monday. A US Marshal would pick her up at noon and return her to the center before three. Meagan was unnerved at the very thought of going into downtown Washington, DC, but the agent assured her that they would take every precaution to ensure that she would be safe.

Her imagination began to run wild. What if they ran into someone in Moe's operation? How could they protect her from this dangerous man who even had policemen on his payroll? The agent emphatically vowed to protect her until she was on a flight back to England.

The week before Meagan was scheduled to leave the rehab, a meeting was held on her behalf to discuss her progress and mental stability: Diamond and Sydney were in attendance. She sat in disbelief as she listened to the fraudulent doctor talk about her case. He talked about her as if she were some sort of an entity, rather than a human being that he'd previously enjoyed performing cunnilingus on. It sickened her to watch, as he sat back in his swivel chair trying to look normal. She watched as he straightened his wrinkled jacket, trying desperately not to make eye contact with her, he continued to ramble on saying, "This is a twenty-year old Caucasian female who came to treatment because of long-term drug abuse and severe neurotic symptoms." Meagan thought, "Who was more neurotic than he? Would text books agree that it was abnormal to perform oral sex on your patients, as a condition of their early release?" This Freud was a fraud!

19

A West Coast Christmas

It was a clear Christmas Eve night in beautiful southern California. The temperature was probably around seventy degrees.

As we drove through my neighborhood we could hear the voices of carolers singing Christmas carols.

The Hines' house was the usual ornamental exhibition of a rooftop Santa, complete with eight reindeer, and a life size nativity scene on the front lawn. I remembered how in years gone by the neighbors complained that it was too much because it overshadowed everyone else's decorations. But I'd always hoped that the Hines' would decorate their house in the same manner every year because it reminded me of when I was a little girl. I loved walking through the community with my parents checking out the beautiful decorations. And the Hines' house was my favorite!

At 6 p.m., Grandpa Clayton and I headed for the airport. Diamond's flight was coming in at 7p.m. and I can't remember who was more excited Grandpa Clayton or I.

Yesterday, we decorated the tree, hung Pomegranate wreaths from all the windows on the front of the house, put up the outdoor lights and filled the house with beautiful flowers, mostly Iris because they are Diamond's favorite flower. In spite of the all the tragic events of the year, Grandpa Clayton and I were both determined that this was going to be a great Christmas!

We watched in awe as Diamond stepped onto the escalator and rode down to the ground floor of the LAX. She looked beautiful in her full-length sheared mink coat. I ran up to her and hugged her tightly, and she hugged me back.

Grandpa Clayton hugged her and kissed her on her forehead. There was so much to talk about and I didn't know where to begin. On the way home, our conversations were scattered, as everyone tried to get in as much as they could. At one point it became so ridiculous that we stopped talking and broke into laughter.

We had a late formal dinner in the dinning room. I used my mother's best china and crystal, and I had Tina help me to prepare the meal. I wanted my grandmother to see how well my mother had trained me in the area of formal entertaining.

After dinner we sang carols and drank eggnog before opening our gifts. Around 12:30 Diamond made the suggestion that we should make the four-hour drive to Grandpa Clayton's home on the reservation.

"Clayton wouldn't it be nice to visit your parents for Christmas? They probably haven't seen Erica since she was a little girl." At that precise moment Clayton knew that he still loved Diamond because she always knew what to do to make others happy.

"That's a great idea but what about Erica? She probably wants to spend some time with her friends."

"Grandpa, I would love to go."

"Are you sure? What about Carl?"

Diamond asked, "Why don't you invite Carl?"

I responded saying, "Carl's grandparents are coming in from Wisconsin and he hasn't seen them for a really long time. So if you don't mind, I would really rather hangout with the two of you: if it's okay?"

Laughing, Diamond said, "It wouldn't be a holiday without our favorite grandchild."

It was agreed that we would leave for the reservation early tomorrow morning.

Diamond awakened us at 5 a.m. to get ready for the drive ahead.

We arrived on the reservation at approximately eleven thirty am on Christmas morning. I was glad that I'd worn a down vest because it was cold and just looking at the snowcapped mountains made it seem even colder.

I thought of how much the Redfern home had changed. It was not at all what I expected. The last time that I'd been to the reservation, my grandparents were living in a small three-bedroom bungalow. But this was the house that Clayton built! I wished Mom and Dad were alive to see this mini mansion of six bedrooms, four and two-half baths, a humongous family room, library, and five other rooms. There was even a butler's pantry in the dining room. At last the Redferns were living large!

After all of the hugging and tears Diamond went into the kitchen to help Grandma Redfern and the other ladies with dinner while the men retired to the family room to watch the football game. This was going to be a good Christmas!

The day after Christmas, Carl invited me to the John Legend and Kayane West show, at the "House of Blues" in LA. His father got the tickets from a pharmaceutical representative who was pushing a new inhaler. When I told my grandparents about the show and that Carl's parents were going, they forgot to give me curfew. I planned to take full advantage of the no curfew situation by having Carl take me to Madison's Christmas Party, after the show.

The show was tight. When it was over we drove back to Carl's house with his parents, and picked up his truck.

We arrived at the party at 1 a. m. Madison greeted us at the door dressed like an old movie star. The vintage Mae West look and the long-stemmed cigarette made her look like a hooker. We followed her into the game room where she very proudly introduced us to Kevin, her new twenty-eight year old boyfriend, whom I recognized from working in one of the men's boutiques at the mall. This creep made it a point to hang out in front of the store and try to hit on every girl passing by. He used the same line on everyone, "You should be making movies. If you're interested, I got connections."

One hour into the party Carl and I noticed that some of our friends had left the game room and gone upstairs. Curiosity got the best of me and I left Carl at the pool table.

I walked upstairs and into the library to find Kevin pushing E pills and weed to Madison's friends. Motioning to me, he called me over and offered me a pill.

He asked me, "Who do you belong to? Does your man tell you how fine you are? If he doesn't you need to give me a chance." I was shocked that Madison heard him and said nothing. In fact she smiled.

"No thanks I don't use drugs".

"That's because you haven't tried mine."

Holding up a little pill he said, "This little pill will make you feel like a million dollars."

Madison said, "Kevin, leave her alone, she doesn't use."

He responded so harshly that I was frightened for her. "Fall back Bitch! I'm not talking to you! Did I ask you for you opinion?"

I looked at my home girl and I couldn't believe what I'd just heard. Was she high? What was wrong with her? Why didn't she ask him to leave? Who did he think he was, talking to her like that?

I called Madison to the bathroom for a time-out session.

We went into powder room on the second level. I sat on the sink and she sat on the toilet with the top down. "Are you okay? Why are you letting him treat you like that?"

"That's just his way of talking. He's actually quite nice."

I looked deep into her eyes and discovered that they were red with dark circles beneath them.

"There's nothing nice about him. Are you using?"

She became defensive "Whatever I'm doing I am in control. The drugs don't control me!!"

"Where is Kennedy? Does she know?"

"Listen up girlfriend, Kennedy is doing her own thing. You are the only one who's still on the innocent tip."

"Is Kennedy using?"

"She's doing weed and E pills if you want to call that using."

"And what are you doing?"

"Damn, Erica you are full of questions but if you must know, Meth! But I am not hooked. It's purely recreational for me."

I couldn't believe it. I turned my back for a minute and my two best friends are drugging.

"Where is Kennedy?"

"She's in the guesthouse with Jamal and I wouldn't disturb her if I were you."

I walked down to the pool house with only the thought of confronting Kennedy about her involvement with drugs, only to find Kennedy and Erin performing oral sex on Jamal and Dillon. The two super jocks were laid back on the sofa while the girls were kneeling down in front of them. It looked as if they had some kind of a contest going on. They never saw me as I tip toed back out of the pool house and made my way back up the path to the main house.

Walking back to the main house I thought about Kennedy and Madison. I honestly didn't know them anymore. In the past Kennedy would never have ventured out so far as to involve herself in an orgy. With STDs' on the rise, what the hell was she thinking?

20

District of Columbia

The holidays ended as quickly as they'd come. Diamond returned to her life in Washington.

The staff purposely left the office decorated so that she could appreciate how beautiful everything looked but somewhere between LA and DC. She'd lost the holiday spirit.

As she perused her calendar, there were meetings and more meetings that she needed to attend on today.

Mid-morning and halfway through dictation Reagan walked into Diamond's office with an exceptionally handsome and well-dressed gentleman, and announced that they were just coming in from Barbados.

Reagan said, "Mrs. Redfern how was your holiday?" Not giving Diamond a chance to respond she went on to say, "My friend and I are just coming in from Barbados. We rented a villa in Christ Church that was absolutely fabulous. I just stopped by to check my schedule for the remainder of the week."

Diamond sat at her cherry-wood desk surrounded by her accomplishments that elaborately decorated the walls of her office. These were only a few of the many memoirs that chronicled her beautiful life. Directly across from her desk was a turn of the century French settee and a butler's table with fresh white Iris flowers. On the back wall under the window there was a fully stocked glass wine cabinet, and to the left a credenza with countless memoirs from her visits to Somalia.

She leaned back in her chair, looking trendy and youthful in her black wool newsboy cap, black and white V cut sweater, black jeans and black and white cowboy boots making it impossible to determine her age.

Moe was definitely caught off guard because if he'd met this woman anywhere other than with Reagan he would definitely have hit on her. She was a rarity, beautiful, classy, sexy and probably rich.

Moe was so intrigued that he didn't hear Reagan when she said, "Diamond I'd like for you to meet Mr. Johnson. Mr. Johnson this is Mrs. Redfern. Mr. Johnson is in real estate and international investing. He also specializes in off-shore prop-erties."

Moe managed to say hello, as he stared in awe of Diamond.

Diamond thought how pretentious Reagan had become, introducing her by her last name and emphasizing the Mrs. in front of her name. She had not forgot-ten how Reagan tried to steal her man. She thought, "I'll give her a little some-thing to be jealous about." After checking out the handsome man with Reagan, she called her secretary into her office and said, "I am expecting an important call from Kurt. Take a message because I don't want to be disturbed."

Ebony responded, "Yes Diamond."

Diamond sat back in her chair and gazed alluringly at Moe. And in her most sexy voice she said, "Mr. Johnson please have a seat. I'd love to talk with you sometime in the near future about the purchase of some beach front property in Ft Lauderdale and perhaps some land in the Bahamas, but at the moment I am overwhelmed with two weeks worth of work in front of me. Why don't you leave your card and I'll call you for an appointment in a few days. Perhaps we can have a working lunch."

Moe didn't have a clue about how to approach the subject of beachfront prop-erty but somehow he managed to wing it. He was undeniably caught off guard, mostly because he was intrigued with Diamond. She was beautiful, interesting, and provocative. He began to search his outer coat, and then the jacket pockets of his suit for his imaginary calling card. And then in his most apologetic voice Moe said, "I'm sorry Mrs. Redfern but I seemed to have left my cards at home."

Reagan who was always one step ahead of the game said, "Darling, you can give your card to me and I'll give it to her another time."

"Thanks Baby." Turning to Diamond, he said, "Mrs. Redfern, I look forward to meeting with you real soon."

Diamond determined to make Reagan jealous by further engaging Mr. Johnson in conversation said, "By the way Mr. Johnson where is your company based?"

Moe stumbling over his words responded, "Aaaat the moment I'm working from my home but my home office is in Chicago."

Now she would really mess with Reagan's head. "Perhaps we could do lunch at your place?" Now that's something that he had not thought of. If he ever got this diva bitch alone he would screw her brains right out of her skull. For a brief moment he had an instant visual of Diamond in a red animal print panty and bra. He smiled as he envisioned her as his love slave or maybe he would entice Reagan to make arrangements for a ménage a trois. He become so aroused that his thoughts began to run wild and it became difficult for him to conceal his erection.

"We can work out the details when you call me. Thanks for your interest, Mrs. Redfern."

"Please call me Diamond."

"And you beautiful lady, may call me Moe."

Reagan wanted to puke as she heard her lover's response to Diamond.

Her facial expression made a marked change as she saw the two gazing lustfully into each other's eyes. It was obvious that she was incensed as they turned to leave Diamond's office. She'd gone in on her day off purposely to make Diamond jealous of her new love interest but it backfired because Moe appeared to be intrigued with Diamond. Now she'd have to think of something to divert his thinking.

As Moe and Reagan were about to exit Diamond's office, Ebony stepped into the office and announced that she had and emergency message from the police commissioner. Moe's ears perked up with the mention of the police commissioner, and he froze in his tracks.

Diamond asked, "What is the message?"

"He called to say that Meagan will be meeting with the Federal prosecutor at 12 noon tomorrow."

"Thanks Ebony. I'll let Sydney know."

Moe's countenance changed, as he heard the name Meagan connected with the police commissioner's. Suddenly it was all coming together. He'd heard

Meagan talk about her uncle's employer, Diamond. Was this the Diamond: the bitch that sent the police looking for Meagan? Suddenly, Diamond lost her appeal to Moe. He very smoothly reached for Diamond's hand and kissed it as if he'd made a love connection, grabbed Reagan's arm and they made a quick dash to the elevator.

At the same time Diamond connected the name Moe Johnson to Meagan. She wasn't a hundred percent sure because of how Erica described him to her. Erica said the man was old and dirty with gold teeth but this man was absolutely gorgeous, impeccably groomed with pretty teeth. If she could get Reagan alone she would be able to find out more.

Reagan and Moe left WBIT together. Moe dropped Reagan at her place on Massachusetts and 14th Street, and told her to pack for a quick trip to New York.
She asked, "But why tonight?"
Moe wanted to say, "Because I said so Bitch" but he had to be careful because he was really in love with Reagan and he didn't want to lose her. You could not disrespect a woman like Reagan Winters. Unlike Meagan she didn't need him because she had everything: brains and beauty. Besides she would be his alibi if he needed one.
"Baby I just want to have you all to myself, before you go back to work."
Reagan feeling vulnerable and unintentionally gullible bought into his explanation. "Okay Moe, I'll pack. What time should I be ready?"
"I should be back in an hour to pick you up."

Moe dropped Reagan off: jumped into his whip and minutes later he was on the phone to his gambling partner Johnny Bop.

Johnny Bop was an old school Italian hood, an FBI (full-blooded Italian) with the right connections. He was what the 'mob' called a 'made man', a Sicilian who still had family and connections in Sicily. He had arranged more than one hundred hits in his lifetime and none had been connected to him.

Moe thought briefly about his own manpower. It had been completely wiped out with the death of Lobo and the disappearance of Alan. When he thought about it he really didn't have anyone that he could depend on to carryout an order. Most of his workers were young with two things on their mind, money and sex. Unlike the others, Alan had been a leader and his best Lieutenant. With

Alan gone, he had only one choice and that was to call on his mob connection. If he'd used better logic he would have initially called on the mob to take Meagan out, and he wouldn't be in this dilemma. From his previous dealings with mob guys, he knew that whenever they got an assignment, they were dead on it until the job was complete. They usually came in town in the morning, handled their business, and were home in time for dinner. For wise guys contract killing was business, sort of like a job without personal attachment.

Moe explained to Johnny that he needed a professional hit and that it had to be done right away.

"Hey Johnny, I need your help right away."

"Moe Baby, what you got for me?"

"Is this phone safe?"

"Nothing is safe until the deal is done. Don't you realize that modern technology has made it that way? Do you remember that old country western song?" Before Moe could respond he began to sing, "You got to know when to hold them. Know when to fold them and count your blessings when the deal is done."

When he finished he said, "Meet me at the old dealing place at three o'clock sharp."

That was Johnny Bop. He was always talking in riddles, or singing: leaving you to read between the lines to follow whatever it was that he was talking about. Johnny Bopp served 10 years in Federal prison for conspiracy to commit murder, and all they really had on him was wiretapping. This was why he was so careful about anything that he said on the phone. Nevertheless, Moe knew exactly where to meet him. He would meet him at Nick's gambling joint in southeast.

Moe arrived first on the scene, laying out his agenda for Johnny. Flashing a picture of Meagan, Moe said, "Look man, I need a real professional to take this Bitch out. She's trying to send me back to prison and I need to put her out of her misery by tomorrow before she has a chance to talk to the federal prosecutor."

Johnny took off his glasses and starred into Moe's eyes, "This is short notice. Where is she now?"

"Man I don't have a clue. If I did I would have already done the job!"

"So tell me, how is my man supposed to get to her?"

"He is going to have to do her either at the courthouse or on her way back home from the courthouse. I know for a fact that she'll be at the federal courthouse tomorrow at noon."

Johnny laughed, "This must be a bad joke."

"Trust me this is about as real as it gets, and I am serious as a heart-attack!"

"Is she in witness protection?"

"That I don't know."

"If she's in the witness protection program she won't be traveling alone. It's very likely there will be a US Marshall with her or a Fed."

"I thought about that and I have every confidence that your man can handle this."

Johnny said, "What if we have to take out the US Marshall? Moe baby, I'd like to help you but this is a very dangerous thing that you are asking. And what if there are two of them?"

"Johnny, why are you trying to play me when I know that you've handled bigger jobs than this? This ought to be small potatoes for your people. What do you think? I'm not good for the cash."

"I know you got the cash."

"So what's the problem?"

"No problem at all. Just don't believe everything that you see on the television. Tony Soprano only exists on television and even if I could get a couple of guys to come in tonight, it's gonna cost you big."

"Like how much?"

"I can't be a hundred per cent sure: Maybe twenty grand for the girl and fifty for the US Marshall.

Moe responded without hesitation, "I can give you half now and half when the job is complete."

Johnny shaking the dice in his hand said, "Better let me make sure I can get my man here by tomorrow."

"How long will it take you to find out? I am leaving for New York tonight and I want to be a million miles away when it goes down."

"I call you later tonight."

21

Meagan's Destiny

It was a bitter cold day in Maryland, as Meagan and her US Marshall left the Rehabilitation Center, and walked to his car. The air smelled clean, the temperature was below freezing but most importantly she was drug-free. She watched as if for the first time, snowflakes falling ever so softly from the sky to make patterns on the ground. As the Marshall helped her into his grey Crown Victoria, the world seemed right again. It was the first time in weeks that Meagan had been in the outside world. She thought "What if Alan and Lobo had been successful at murdering her? What if Diamond had not taken an interest in her well being and found a rehab for her?" She was grateful that Diamond had sent the detectives to find her and she was very thankful that Moe was not successful in his attempt to have her murdered.

When she thought about it she had not had a real friend since she came to this country. All of the people that she'd come in to contact had used and abused her. Now that she'd had time to think she realized that Diamond was a friend, probably her best friend.

There were icy road conditions and the marshal called ahead to say that they would be arriving one hour later than they planned. As they drove east on interstate 70, a tractor-trailer jackknifed causing the marshal's car to slide off the road and down an icy embankment into a tree. Meagan was dazed as she freed herself from the wreckage. Minutes later the marshal crawled from his smoking car. Meagan bleeding from the head and the marshal with apparent collarbone injuries were flown by medivac to the shock-trauma unit in downtown Baltimore.

Jason Johnson sat in his office on the 10th floor of the federal building awaiting the arrival of his star witness. He'd done his homework and he felt he had enough evidence to put Moe away for the rest of his life. At 1 p.m., he got the news about the accident. At 1:05pm he was on the phone with the Fed's. The federal agent asked, "Why wasn't she placed in one of our federal relocation sites? What the hell was she doing in a plush rehab in Maryland? Now all of our fucking work is down the drain. We could have nailed Moe Johnson's ass to the wall today!"

Jason responded, "Sir it's not like she's a fatality. She will live to testify another day."

A few weeks later Meagan and her US Marshall entered through the back of the courthouse and took the service elevator to the 15th floor. The interview and meeting with the grand jury took exactly 90 minutes to complete. As she left the courtroom, she looked long into the eyes of the young federal prosecutor, as if she was looking for some guarantee that Moe would be put away forever. She needed assurance that she would never have to see Moe Johnson again.

She was on crutches as she boarded British Airways flight 5667 for London but it was not until the plane took off that she felt safe from the clutches of Moe. In fact it was the first time that she'd felt safe in months.

22

New York Big City of Dreams

Moe waited most of the afternoon for a call from Johnny to let him know that Meagan ceased to exist. With her out of the way he could move on with his life.

At 4 p.m., he left Reagan in the hotel room and headed downstairs to use one of the phones in the lobby. Johnny Bop answered on the first ring.

"Hey Johnny, what's up?"

"Moe Baby, I'm going to give you another number to call me." Moe jotted the number down and called Johnny back within seconds.

"Man I've been waiting all afternoon to hear from you. I need to know something."

"All I can tell you is that my men waited until 3 o'clock and that your girl didn't show. Are you sure that you got the right information?"

"Yea I'm sure. Are you sure that your men where on point? You know, in position."

"The two guys that I sent are natural born assassins and they don't make mistakes. Maybe there was a change in plans."

"Man, I'm telling you that this was a sure thing. The message came down from the police commissioner himself."

"Man, I didn't know that you were connected like that."

"It's a long story." Moe suddenly didn't feel like talking anymore. He cut the conversation short saying: "Johnny let me get back to you on this."

"Okay Moe, whenever you're ready."

Moe was devastated. How would he keep Meagan from testifying against him? Where was she? Why the fuck was she so hard to kill!" He walked slowly through the lobby of the hotel and into the bar area where he sat down and called Reagan to join him.

Reagan walked across the lobby of the Marriott Marquise in a white cashmere coat with fur accents. All eyes on where on her as she glided across the floor like a Parisian runway model.

Looking at his beautiful lady, Moe momentarily forgot his troubles and focused on her.

As she neared the table he rose from his seat. Then he took her by the hand and led her out of the hotel where he hailed a cab.

"Moe, where are we going?"

"It's a surprise."

She smiled, "This trip has been full of surprises."

"Have I disappointed you?"

"Oh no Baby, I can't think of any place I'd rather be."

Moe told the cab driver to take them to Tiffany's. Reagan's assumption was that Moe was purchasing another expensive piece of jewelry for her.

Once inside the store Moe asked the clerk to show them a selection of diamond engagement rings. Reagan couldn't believe what she'd heard but she decided to act indifferent about it. The jeweler returned with two selections of diamond and platinum rings, one pricey and a less pricey selection. Moe asked Reagan to choose from one of the selections.

"Moe what does this ring mean?"

"It means that I love you, and I want to marry you."

Reagan was taken back and lost for words.

"But Moe it hasn't been long enough. What I mean is that we haven't known each other long enough!"

Moe said, "Long enough for what? Long enough for whom? Do you love me Reagan?"

"Of course I love you Moe. That's not the problem."

The jeweler not wanting to lose the sale nervously asked if they needed some time alone. Moe told the man no. He took Reagan by the hand, kissed her on the lips and asked, "Reagan Winters will you be my wife?"

It was all happening so fast. Reagan had been caught completely off guard. How much did she really know about this man? She had not even met his mother! Reagan really needed to talk to her best friend Diamond but she remembered that they were no longer best friends. In fact she couldn't think of anyone else other than Diamond that she could talk to about this. Diamond would be the rational thinker and as usual she would go along with whatever Diamond thought to be best. She felt like she did at seventeen when she was asked to give up her virginity, without anyone to confide in.

"Moe I need more time."

"How much time do you need?"

Right about now time was a major factor in the equation. She was almost forty and she'd never been married so it was probably now or never. Why was she being hesitant? He was finer than wine, the sex was superb and the man had money. What else could she have asked for?

"Oh alright Moe, I will marry you."

As she tried on ring after ring, a handsome young couple walked in. The handsome young man requested to pick up a ring he previously ordered. When the young man's eyes met Moe's he acted as if he'd seen a ghost. It was Tricia and Alan. Moe got up from his chair saying, "Hey Alan! Where have you been?" He extended his hand for a handshake.

Alan was trembling with fear as he extended his hand, "No where man", as he grabbed his girl by the arm and headed for the door, with the clerk walking fast behind them: to inquire as to when they would be back to pick up their 6 carat canary yellow diamond ring.

Reagan asked Moe, "What was that about?"

"The guy owes me some money and I guess he doesn't intend to pay me."

"Is he afraid of you? He looked sacred to death."

He pulled her close and kissed her softly on the lips, "Now why would anyone be afraid of me?"

Reagan quickly forgot the incident and continued to try on engagement rings.

Reagan and Moe were married a week later by a justice of the peace in Stowe Vermont. Reagan wanted a Mediterranean Cruise as a honeymoon but Moe insisted on something simple and somewhere stateside. He promised his beautiful bride, "We can take our real honeymoon in late spring. I promise we'll go any-where in the world that makes you happy. But for right now I need to stay close to home. You know for business reasons."

The Honeymoon suite at the luxurious Vermont resort was incredible. On the first day at the resort, they spent all morning in the spa salon. In the evening they took a carriage ride by moonlight. The next day they slept in, and breakfast was served to them in bed at their villa: and bed is where they spent the next five days of absolute bliss.

23

Finer than Wine

A few weeks later Moe and Reagan gave a banging reception at a hotel in 'Crystal City.' Diamond insisted that I fly to DC for the reception because Reagan wanted me as one her hostess. Because the reception was held during 'Spring Break' it worked out for me.

It was the supposed to be the reception of the decade. Moe looked handsome and debonair, sort of like a modern day Prince Charming, in his black Gucci Tux. While Reagan looked like the winner of the Miss World pageant: in an off white asymmetrical strapless satin gown, with filigree gold embroidered bolero jacket.

All of the right people were in attendance, even Diamond and the Judge.

When Diamond came through the reception line looking as if she were about to steal the show, it took every ounce of restraint for Reagan to maintain her composure. This was her day, and she refused to let Diamond upstage her. When she and Moe danced the first dance of the evening, to Etta James 'At Last', Reagan looked up at Moe and very dramatically kissed him long and hard, until the guests began to applaud them. Unfortunately, Diamond and the Judge had stepped onto the veranda and missed the show that was put on especially for them.

Special guests were served 1978 Dom Perignon and all others were served Moet. Every female guest was given a Tiffany's bracelet while the males were given a box of expensive Cuban cigars.

The floral arrangements were beautiful and exotic. The menu was fit for royalty: a crusted filet mignon, tomatoes marsci, salmon wrapped in lettuce leaves, sautéed calamari and shrimp, mixed greens, herb racks of lamb, vegetarian pasta, and ambrosia for dessert.

Midway through the reception, I decided to take a break. I walked out into the lobby looking for a little privacy so that I could relax for a moment. The truth is that the five-inch stilettos that I was wearing were killing my feet.

I strolled out into the lobby and walked smack into Justin Black and I was instantly traumatized by his presence. What I could not fathom was what was this low-life doing at Reagan's reception? He was the last person that I'd expected to see at Reagan's reception. He was definitely out of his league.

Half stumbling over my words, and projecting a manufactured smile, I managed to say, "Hello Justin, I didn't know that you would be here."

With a cynical look on his face Justin said, "Look Shortie, don't play me. You know that wherever my man Moe is, I'm right behind him."

I could tell that he was still fuming about me standing him up.

In disbelief, I asked, "Do you mean that Moe was invited?" Moe is here?"

Justin answered, "Invited? He's the guest of honor."

Now I'm for sure this idiot is crazy because Reagan Winters would never invite someone like Moe to her reception. Reagan Winters the socialite wouldn't be caught dead with someone of Moe's character. I asked, "Why are you saying this? What business would Moe have here?"

"When you go back inside, I want you to take a good look at your friend's new husband. Yeah, my man has stepped up his game but underneath the flash and the bling-bling, he is still my man Moe."

I was shocked. "Are you telling me that this is the same man that you sent me to pick up the money for your bond? This Moe person is Reagan's husband?"

"That's exactly what I'm saying."

"But Reagan wouldn't give someone like that the time of day."

He laughed, "Maybe not but she married him. Just take a good look at the groom when you go back inside."

I used his comment as a chance to exit his presence by saying, "It was nice to see you again. Call me sometime."

"Hold up shortie. We got some unfinished business between us."

I said, "Why don't I call you later. I am sort of working right now."

He was really angry when he blocked my path and said, "Who the fu-k do you think you playing with? And if you don't know, you better ask somebody cause don't no Bitch play me and walk away!!!!!!"

I felt that he was way out of line in his approach to me, and I wasn't having it! As I turned to walk back into the ballroom, Justin grabbed me, pulled me into a corner and kissed me. I tried to free myself from his grip but he was too strong. The next thing that I remember, he was slipping one hand under my dress and then down into my thong. He whispered, with his lips touching mine, "So you still a virgin?" His hand was pressing hard against my vulva and with his middle finger he began rubbing my clitoris. I tried to scream but he covered my mouth with his. Next he pushed me to the floor. Holding me down with his muscular body, he took his hand out of my thong and began to lick his fingers. "Damn baby, I got to have you. Can I have you?" I think he would have gone much further if he had not been interrupted at that moment.

"Justin, what the hell are you doing?" It was Nicky. Lucky for me he'd brought her to the reception as his guest because she showed up at the right time. He was stunned by her presence and released his grip on me. I broke free and got up from the cold hard marble floor and straightened my dress.

Justin was heated. "The last time I checked my mother was in Alabama. How many times do I have to tell you about interfering with my business? Go back inside, or else I will put you in cab and send your ass home."

I managed to say, "Nicky I am so sorry."

"No need for you to apologize. I saw the whole thing! It was Justin acting as if he wanted to rape you. And guess what we made love this morning."

Justin got in Nicky's face, "Bitch, I know that you did not put me out there like that. And didn't I tell you to stop following me?"

Nicky said, "You put yourself out there. I do everything for you and this is how you repay me? Justin Black if you weren't the father of my son … I would"

"You would do what?" He slapped her so hard that he left his handprint on her olive colored cheek. With blood gushing from her nose, Nicky ran outside of the hotel, and I ran back into the reception area.

Although, I wasn't physically hurt, I was upset and stunned about the way that Justin had handled me. No one had ever forced himself on me as he had. And besides that, what if he told someone that he knew me, and it got back to Diamond. Even worse, what if Moe recognized me? I needed to get out of there ASAP.

As I made my way back into the reception, I stopped momentarily near the head table and gave Reagan's husband a short but intense look. It was really Moe!

I couldn't believe the transformation of this man. He'd gone from an old scrubby low-life man to a handsome middle age stud. But what I could not understand was what was Reagan doing with a drug-dealer? I wondered if she'd ever visited him in that horrible apartment building. Suddenly nothing made sense anymore!

Near the point of hysteria, I made my way through the crowd and back to Diamond.

I was near frantic when I told Diamond that we needed to leave right away.

"Calm down Erica and tell me why? Why do we need to leave?"

I could hardly talk "It's him!"

"It's who? Who are you talking about?"

"Reagan's husband is the one."

"Erica calm down and tell me. What about Reagan's husband?"

"The man is Meagan's friend. Don't you remember the drug dealer that I told you about?"

"Of course I remember. He has the same name but this is not the man that you described."

"Well he must have had a makeover but I'm for sure that this is the man".

"After seeing him only once, how can you be sure?"

"You've got to believe me. It's really him!"

I was talking incessantly with Diamond, trying to convince her that Reagan's husband was the drug-dealer that I'd met last summer, when I became distracted by Nicky's reappearance in the ballroom. She looked elegant in her sky blue satin pants suit and she walked with the grace and ease of a gazelle: almost as if in slow motion. Our eyes met momentarily and I still remember that the luster was gone from hers. It was almost as if the lights had been turned out. Still I could not believe that she'd comeback to the reception. Hadn't she had enough of Justin? Why didn't she get the message that he was real-life walking scum? What did he have to do for her to get the message?

I watched as Nicky confronted Justin. It appeared that they were arguing. Suddenly I heard three shots fired simultaneously, and without really seeing what happened, I knew that Nicky had shot Justin. Everything that followed seemed to happen in a blur, as the crowd broke into ear piercing screaming and scattering.

Diamond and the Judge gathered their belongings along with me, and we were whisked away in our limo before the news media arrived. Once inside the stretch, Diamond started hugging me as if I was an infant and Burton was hugging her.

As soon as I could catch my breath and digest what just happened, I continued to tell Diamond about Reagan's husband.

With the mention of Moe's name the Judge perked up: taking note as if he were awaiting the verdict from a jury.

Diamond asked, "Erica, are you one hundred per cent sure because you cannot afford to make a mistake about something like this."

"Grandmother, I am one hundred and ten per cent sure."

"Burton, there is only one thing to do and that is to call Kurt. This is his area of expertise."

Burton very sarcastically said, "Lets' hope he's sober enough to understand what you're talking about."

Diamond called her friend Kurt the District's police commissioner from the car.

Kurt was very sober when he got the call from Diamond: he thanked her, and at the end of the day he took all the credit for tracking and arresting the notorious Moses Johnson. We watched the late night news as Moe was escorted from his reception in handcuffs, with Reagan walking frantically behind in her wedding dress.

Nicky appeared in a later newscast in her sky blue pantsuit, that was now covered in blood. The news commentator announced that she was being held without bail for the alleged first-degree murder of her boyfriend. They said that the victim's name was being withheld until the next of kin had been notified.

I could not believe that Nicky killed Justin. What was she thinking? What about her baby? Even more I wondered about Justin's last thoughts. I wondered if he knew that I would be the last person that he would ever kiss on this earth. Somehow I felt responsible. Maybe if I hadn't led Justin on, he would not have been angry enough to try to rape me, and Nicky would not have shot him. Was it my fault that Justin was dead?

Later that evening, I overheard Diamond on the phone with Christen saying, "Get a hold of Reagan right away and tell her that we need to meet with her tonight."

Christen said, "But tonight is her special night. Can't this wait until tomorrow?"

Diamond's demeanor changed as she said, "Didn't you watch the news? Her husband has been arrested and she's probably home alone."

Diamond was pacing the floor, walking back and forth, without breaking a stride. I can't ever remember seeing her so intense.

"We can't afford to bring negative publicity to the station. Tell her not to talk to anyone and that we will take care of the media for her: Starting with the fact that she married Moe under false pretense. Yes, that's it: the man misrepresented himself as a real-estate developer from the Mid West, and she plans to have the marriage annulled right away."

Christen said, "What if she doesn't feel the way that you think she does?"

"She's a very intelligent person and I am sure that these are her sentiments as well."

Christen asked, "But what if they aren't her sentiments?"

"Then we will have to find away to convince her to do what is best for the business."

Christen and Sydney somehow managed to get Reagan to come to Diamond's house at midnight but to no avail because Reagan was determined to stand by her man. She'd spent two hours at the police station and another hour with Moe's attorney, so last thing that she needed was a lecture from Diamond.

Diamond started off by saying, "Reagan dear, we want you to know how sorry we are that this happened to you, especially on what should have been the happiest day of your life. And we certainly understand how you must feel." The others in the room nodded, as though in agreement with Diamond. Reagan still dressed in her reception gown with her clustered curls falling loosely around her head said, "How could any of you understand? It didn't happen to you. Anyway I won't believe any of this until my husband tells me the facts." Christen began to speak as the legal representation for the station. "We understand how you feel about your husband, and we deeply sympathize with you, but you need to be reasonable about this."

Reagan sat down in utter disbelief as she listened to Diamond and Christen make plans about how they would handle the media if the story about Reagan's marriage to Moe got out.

Reagan was angry. Angry because they were talking about ending her marriage to a man that she truly loved, as if she had nothing to say in the matter. With tears in her eyes she said, "Moe and I are together because I love him and because we fit. I married him for better or worse and if you think that I'm going to turn my back on the only man whoever truly loved me, you can forget it! Sydney, please take me home!"

Diamond said, "Okay Reagan, let's be reasonable and think about your future."

"Diamond, why don't you cut the bullshit? You could care less about my future but you do care about the station. And right about now I don't give shit about the station."

"Reagan you are wrong because I care very much about your future."

"If you care about my future, back-off and leave me the hell alone!!!!!!!!"

"Reagan Dear, I wish that I could allow you to work this out on your own but the matter is bigger than you. It involves the livelihood of every employee at the station."

"That's where you are wrong because the matter is between my husband and me."

Diamond said, "I know that you feel a sense of loyalty to Moe but you have to realize that he is not the man that you thought he was. The man is nothing more than a common hood: A drug-dealer!"

Reagan screaming and crying saying, "Don't you dare talk to me about who he is? You don't know him!"

"Now you listen to me Reagan Winters. I have tried to be reasonable with you. Now I'm offering you two ultimatums: either you prepare a formal state-ment for the media to include plans to have your marriage annulled, or resign from WBIT!"

Reagan began to cry, "It's not that simple. I think that I'm pregnant."

Christen said, "You can't be serious. Surely you are going to abort it?"

Reagan stood to her feet as if she were going to physically attack Christen for making what she considered to be a callous remark "You Bitch! If I am pregnant, that means that this baby is a part of me! How can you talk about disposing of my baby: as if it where a piece of garbage?"

Christen trying to clean up her insensitivity said, "Okay girl, I apologize. Please forgive me."

Diamond asked, "Are you going to keep the baby or give it up for adoption?"

"I don't know what I'm going to do but I do know that I love my husband."

Diamond in a condescending tone said, "Of course you love him but you need to think of your future and remember that he deceived you. Chances are he is going away for a very long time. You need to disassociate yourself from Moe Johnson, and you need to do it publicly for the good of all of us."

Reagan began crying non-stop but managed to say, "Why do I need to denounce him? Is it because of the bad publicity that it might bring to your precious station?" Everyone looked at each other knowing full well that this was the reason that Diamond called the meeting.

Diamond motioned for Sydney to meet her in the next room, where she asked him to run to the 24-hour drugstore to get a pregnancy test kit for Reagan. Diamond thought that if Reagan did not have a pregnancy to worry about, they could probably persuade her to see Moe for what he really was.

Sydney asked, "Is there a specific brand that I should get?"

"Sydney, I haven't been pregnant in thirty-seven years and that makes me clueless about the brands. Just ask the pharmacist for the one with the most reliability."

When Diamond returned to the room she placed her arm around Reagan's shoulder and asked, "Where is Moe? Was he at home when you left?"

Reagan said, "No he had important business to take care of."

"Reagan I want you to listen to yourself? What could possibly be more important than being with you on the night of your wedding reception?"

We sat patiently around the dining table waiting for the results of the pregnancy test.

And it was Diamond who fainted when the test results revealed that Reagan was pregnant.

24

Revenge

Moe was out on a two million dollar bail bond. The federal prosecutor argued that he might be a flight risk but his lawyer's convinced the court that Moe was a married man with a baby on the way, and with definite ties to the community and there was no danger of his fleeing the country.

Moe had two alternatives: one was to take the federal prosecutor out before his trial date, and the other was to make a monetary deal with him. Once he found out the prosecutor's daily routine, he sent Carlo his personal private detective as his negotiator, to make an offer of one hundred thousand dollars.

"Carlo I want you to make him an offer of one hundred grand. If he takes it I want to know right away. If he doesn't I want to know that as well."

Later that evening Carlo called Moe.

"Yeah Moe I spoke to the federal prosecutor. He laughed at your offer and told me that if I came back again, I would be doing time for attempting to bribe a federal prosecutor."

Moe said, "I don't give a damn what he said. I want you to talk to him again, and this time I want you to offer him two hundred grand. I know his punk ass will bite for that kind of cash."

"Moe I'm trying to tell you that this one is straight. He is straight all the way and he isn't going to go for it."

"Man what the hell am I paying you for. It's your job to convince him. What did you find out about his background? Is he married? Does he have kids?"

"No wife and no kids, and yes he lives alone."

"No wife and no kids and he lives alone but he does have a mother and a girl-friend? Or even better does he have a boyfriend?"

"He's a real pretty-boy alright, and he's got a pretty girl. In fact he is supposed to get married next month."

Moe asked, "Does his girl live with him?"

"No she lives out of town: somewhere in the south."

"Get me the 411 on her: just in case all else fails."

"You got it Moe."

Carlo scoped out the prosecutor's daily routine for nearly a month. The man was so damned predictable. After work he went straight to the gym. Dinner was usually a salad from whole foods and weather permitting he went bike riding afterwards in Rock Creek Park. He attended church regularly and on two occasions he stopped for happy hour with his co-workers.

On the evening that Carlo set out to make his last and final offer to the prosecutor, he suited up for a workout and headed for the gym.

The gym was unusually crowded for a mid-week night but it didn't take long for him to find Jason. Carlo took notice that this bronze Adonis was very serious about his workout. There were a few superfine women who stopped by to speak with Jason, as he carried out his daily exercise ritual but he appeared nonchalant and stepped up his workout. He was not a player.

As the prosecutor stepped on to the treadmill and began the last part of his workout Carlo said, "Hey man did you give anymore thought to the offer that I made you."

No! And I don't like to be disturbed during my workout"

"Mr. Johnson told me to offer you two-hundred grand and promises that you'll never hear from him again."

"I 'm not interested."

'Did you hear me? He is offering you two hundred grand. The money will be deposited into a Swiss bank, or any bank, in whoever's name you want it in."

25

The Resurrection of Justin Black

It was prom time and everyone was making such a fuss about what to wear, who to be seen with and what to do after the prom. Of course Kennedy and I made the decision not to eat at the prom but to have our dates take us to the Belmont Hotel for dinner, afterwards. Later into the evening we would attend Bethany's party at her mansion in Beverly Hills. The night was going to be perfect: including a chauffer driven limousine for the entire night.

After visiting practically every gown and bridal shop in LA, I finally decided on a strapless red-cuffed gown with black sequins and a black shawl. Kennedy decided on the opposite, a black gown with red sequins. The dresses were a perfect fit, which meant we could not afford to binge on anything until after the prom.

The evening that Diamond flew in, we were out shopping for shoes when I got a call around 7 p.m. This was the call that would forever change my life: bringing about an end to my youthful innocence: at least as far as my grandmother was concerned.

Diamond said, "Erica. What time are you coming home?"

I detected that something was wrong because I didn't hear the usual cheery quality in her voice. Her voice was slightly off-key, as if she were irritated.

"Hello Grandmother, is something wrong? Kennedy and I are shopping for shoes to match our prom dresses. I should be home around 9 p.m.: unless you need me now."

"I need to talk to you right away and it is very important. You can shop for shoes tomorrow!"

"Can you tell me what it's about?"

I knew it couldn't be anything school related because I was a model student. I thought, maybe something happened to one of her friends and she needed to talk to me about it. Or maybe she'd made a decision about Burton and my Grandfather. But why did she sound so upset?

Diamond said that the young woman who had been accused of the murder at Reagan's wedding had said that I was involved to a certain degree because minutes before the murder, she'd witnessed Justin Black, the deceased young man, attempting to rape me. She said that if she had not intervened that he would have raped me. She further divulged that the deceased was her fiancée'. The young woman was Nicky and she was pleading insanity: needing my testimony to back her up. Suddenly, I didn't feel like shopping anymore. I felt a devastating sensation throughout my body and my stomach was in knots. I didn't know how to respond. How could I possibly be involved? I didn't have any part in Justin's murder.

"Okay, I am on my way home."

When I arrived home Diamond was in the library. She appeared calm but I knew it was just a ploy to have me feel comfortable enough to tell all and then she would lean on me. I was glad that Grandpa Clayton was out when she began her interrogation. It would have been real embarrassing to have to discuss the sordid details of Justin's sexual assault on me in his presence. Diamond sat back in my father's chair and with a stern look on her face she said, "Erica let's start at the beginning. How do you know Nicky and Justin?" I put my head down, as if I were searching the floor for answers.

I thought that I'd put all of this behind me but here it was again: following me clear across the country. Justin was dead but somehow he'd been resurrected and he'd caught up with me. Out of the blue I recalled a sermon that I heard last summer entitled "Be Sure Your Sins Will Find You Out!"

Diamond spoke in her most demanding tone, "Erica I want you to sit down and look at me when I talk to you, and most importantly I want the truth."

I was trying to understand why was Diamond talking to me as if I were on trial? I wondered if she would she still think of me in the same way, or would the relationship change when she found out the truth? I felt my heart fluttering around in my chest, as told of the first night I'd met Justin Black. I didn't know how much Nicky had told so I decided to leave Moe Johnson's name out of the equation along with the fact that I'd been paid five thousand dollars for unknowingly trafficking drugs.

"Erica, I want to know why you didn't feel comfortable enough to tell me at the wedding, that Justin attempted to rape you."

"It was such a happy occasion that I didn't want to ruin it for Reagan."

"Let me reiterate what you just said. A young man that you say you hardly know attempts to rape you and don't tell because you don't want to ruin Reagan's wedding. Erica, just because I am your grandmother doesn't mean that I'm senile!"

"I didn't say that I didn't know him."

"What are you saying Erica? And how do you know Nicky?"

"I met Nicky a day or two after I met Justin."

I was nervous as I thought, how much did Diamond know? I had to think fast "Anyway we ran into her at the Mazda Galleria and she told me to leave her man alone."

"And did you?"

"Of course I did. Only he kept calling me."

Diamond looked me straight in the eyes as if she were trying to decide if I was telling the truth and then she said, "Somehow I think Meagan is involved. Am I right?"

"Yes Justin and Meagan were friends"

"I knew it. Thank Goodness, we are rid of her."

She seemed to experience some relief, to be able to blame what happened on Meagan.

"I spoke with the State's Attorney and with Nicky's attorney. Your testimony will be a major deciding factor in her case. I told them that you would be in DC the last week in June and they agreed to postpone the trial until then. You do understand that you will be under oath and you will have to tell the truth."

I was paralyzed with fear because I'd never had any dealings with the court system, except to go to court to observe my father, whenever he had a well-publicized case. My mind began to think irrationally, "What if Nicky decided to tell the prosecutors about me delivering drugs to her house for Justin? No she wouldn't do that because that would implicate her as the recipient.

I wondered how much Nicky had told her attorney. I wondered if the lawyers would juxtapose our testimonies to see who was telling the truth. I'd rather die than have Diamond find out the truth. There was only one thing to do and that was to talk to Nicky and find out how much she'd revealed to her lawyer.

A month passed and I flew back to Washington, for Nicky's trial. I wore a navy blue 'Lafayette suit and a blue and white pin-stripped shirt to court. Diamond said I should look professional just in case I was called to testify on Nicky's behalf.

Nicky had made the decision to bypass a jury trial, leaving her fate in the hands of Judge Ivy Sherrard. I listened intently as the Judge asked Nicky to rise for sentencing. I gazed across the courtroom, as Nicky stood tall with her head in the air, as if whatever her fate was to be, she was resigned to it. She glowed with an unusual sense of calm while her parents and sisters sat directly behind her holding hands.

I was petrified as Judge Ivy rendered her verdict, "Although, sexual assault is a despicable crime and should not go unpunished, you Nicky Cheryl Simms had no right to take the law into your own hands."

I couldn't breathe. Nicky was going to jail or maybe to her death and it was all because of me. Judge Ivy continued after a long pause, "However, this court has reviewed all of the circumstances surrounding your case. Taking into consideration that you've had no prior dealings with the criminal justice system, it is at this time Nicky Cheryl Simms, I find you not guilty by reason of temporary insanity. The courtroom fell apart as sounds of joy, and cries of pain resonated in the courtroom.

The judge hammered her gavel twice attempting to gain order in the courtroom. Justin's mother broke down in a wail of tears and other members of his family stormed from the courtroom enraged by the verdict.

The Judge continued, "As a part of your release I am ordering you to continue psychiatric counseling with the Pratt group for a period of one year. I am also ordering you to return to a University or college as a full-time student, and you are also mandated to attend parenting classes at the Ruth Center for women every Saturday afternoon for one year. You will be will assigned a social worker appointed by this court, who will monitor your obligatory conditional release. Please see the clerk on your way out.

Nicky with tears streaming down her face very humbly said, "Thank you, your Honor."

Judge Ivy said, "You are free to go, and I hope never to see you in this court-room again."

Everyone was stunned by the incredulous verdict that Judge Ivy rendered: that is everyone except Diamond. It didn't take me long to figure out that Judge Ivy Sherrard and Diamond were good friends and that the 'Ruth Center' where Nicky was assigned parenting classes was Diamond's favorite charity. Diamond was going to make sure that Nicky kept her part of the agreement.

Nicky through a miracle was free. She would never spend another day in jail for Justin's murder. But I wasn't free! Because everyday I blamed myself for Justin's death.

26

The senior class trip

Our senior class trip for this year was to Barcelona, Spain for five days and then on to Malta for six days. Madison and Kennedy, my two best friends, were going with me. It was going to be slamming!

The week before we left, Madison called to say that her boyfriend Kevin had insisted on going with us, and that he given her and ultimatum. She couldn't go if he didn't. When Kennedy found out she was livid. She decided that she would put an end to Kevin and Madison, or at least until after the trip.

Around 6 p.m., the following evening, Kennedy called Kevin and told him that she needed 25 E-pills, an ounce of weed, couple caps of cocaine and some meth for the trip. Because she was placing such a large order, he wanted to know if she was having a bon-voyage party and if so, was he invited? She told him she needed the dope to take on the trip.

"Hey Kevin, I need to score before the trip. It's a big order. Can you deliver?"

"Just how do you plan to get that all that shit through customs?"

Lying she said, "Man you don't need to worry about me I've done this before besides the gang will be splitting it up."

"Okay just tell me where to meet you. Or maybe I could come by your house. I promise to give you a good price if you tighten me up." She hated him, and sex with him was the last thing on her mind.

"No you can't come to my house. My parents are at home. Why don't I meet you at the Arcade at eight? Maybe we can get together afterwards at my cousin's place."

"That sounds hot. Just don't tell Madison or anyone else that you're meeting me. I want you to come alone."

"Why do you want me to come alone?"

"I don't trust those rich kids that you and Madison hang out with."

145

He wanted her to come alone because he planned to have his friend Ethan rob her as soon as she left the arcade. What he hadn't counted on is that Kennedy had plans of her own.

Kevin arrived at the arcade at half past eight and Kennedy was there to greet him. The two went to a nearby table to make the transaction.

As soon as they sat down, he let his hand wander underneath her skirt and up her inner thigh. She laughed, pushed his hand away and said, "Can't you wait?"
He smiled as he said, "I've been waiting too long for you."
"But what about Madison?"
"What about her?"
"Well she is my friend and your girlfriend."
"I'd drop her junkie ass in a minute for you. You're the one that I want!"
He reached under the table for her hand and placed it on his erect penis.
"This could be all yours. All you gotta to do is give me the word and I would drop Madison in a heartbeat."
The thought of being with him made her want to puke but she had to play the game. Pulling her hand away she said, "Let me think about it."

As soon as the money and the drugs were exchanged, and the two were about to leave: two under cover cops came out of nowhere and took both Kennedy and Kevin into custody.
Kevin was booked on several charges. They stemmed from possession, distribution, and the manufacturing of drugs. He was looking at a minimum of five to fifteen.

Little did he know that Kennedy set him up, and that while he was being booked, she was at home packing for the senior class trip to Europe.

We were one hundred strong, from the United States, infiltrating Barcelona: it was awesome. On our first day in Spain we decided to go to Port Ventura theme and water-park. It was there while standing in-line that we met Pablo, and Jacques. Pablo was heir to the Pompey Hotel Chain and he was **actually one of** the most adorable guys that I'd ever met. I asked myself, "How charming and good-looking could one guy be." We were feeling each other from the start.

Jacques on the other hand was equally as attractive but rather shy. He was French born and on vacation in Europe. He'd just graduated Princeton and landed a job on Wall Street working in stocks, and other wealth making commodities. And if ever there were a case of opposites attracting, it was this thing between Kennedy and Jacques. I could tell from the aura around them that they were destined to be. My gut feeling was that she would not be returning to the states with the class.

Jacques and Pablo booked passage on our ship and followed us to Malta. Arm in arm we strolled along the cobblestone streets of Valletta until we found the perfect ring for Kennedy, inside the Savoy Galleria. Afterwards we toured the city checking out the Renaissance art and architecture. Pablo had the hook-up, as he arranged for his brother, who was one of the Parish priests, to perform the ceremony on the next day.

That night the four of us celebrated the engagement of Jacques and Kennedy in our stateroom. We ordered lots of food and champagne. The champagne was more than I could handle and I ended up passing out. When I awakened in the morning, I was lying on the sofa fully dressed with the worst of the worst headaches, and Kennedy was sort of shaking me.

"Girl, get up and get showered."

"My head is killing me. I need some aspirin."

"I'll send for some aspirin, while you shower."

"Why are we in such a hurry?"

"Did you forget? Today is my wedding day."

"Are you sure about this?"

"Of course I'm sure. Today my name changes to Mrs. Jacques Auclair."

"The name sounds fabulous but what about graduation?"

"Tell my Dad to accept my diploma."

"Get serious. You know that your parents are going to go crazy when they find out."

"Maybe not, especially when they find out what he's worth. Anyway, I'm hoping that I'll convince him that we should live in LA."

"Are you marrying him for his money?"

"Don't be ridiculous. But if you really want to know it's because he won't have sex with me unless we're married."

"Are you serious?"

"Plus he calls me a goddess and it sure sounds better than bitch."

"Where will you live?"

"We haven't really decided?"

"When will I see you again?"

"We can talk everyday. Just don't change your cell number."

"I think you need to go back home and discuss this with your family."

"My family will understand."

"No they won't!"

"Maybe not at first but they'll get use to it. Anyway my Dad always said that I'd be a great trophy wife."

"I think he meant after you graduated college."

"Whatever. It's a done deal. So stop trying to talk me out of it."

Kennedy and Jacques married on the steps of St John's Basilica in Malta. Could this possibly be a match made in heaven: A Jewish American Princess and a French born, Seventh-day Adventist? "What should I tell your parents?"

"Tell them that, I'll call them soon."

There was hell to pay for all of us, when our plane landed at the LAX and Kennedy was not on board. Her parent's were irate, refusing to believe that she'd married and made the decision to remain in Europe. They threatened to sue the school, the airline, and the cruise ship unless they could produce their daughter.

A handful of photographers and police came to school the following day to interview everyone regarding Kennedy's disappearance. Once I talked to the police and showed them pictures of the bride and groom in wedding attire, they seemed convinced that there was no foul play involved, and that Kennedy was of age to make her own decisions.

27

"That's All"

It was the end of June and we were about three days away from Shanae's wedding. My main girl Shanae Bugatch was marrying Jason Michael Johnson a federal prosecutor. The wedding was on without a glitch. What a dream come true for Shanae. The bridal party was awesome. It was going to be a garden wedding with sixteen beautiful bridesmaids and sixteen gorgeous groomsmen. In fact it was going to be down right mythical, including ice sculptures, doves and a horse drawn carriage. The groomsmen were lawyers and federal agents and the girls were Shanae's sorority sisters. I couldn't believe that I was going to be a part of it.

Forty miles away in Baltimore's Little Italy, Moe Johnson was making plans of his own. He was meeting with Vesurio and Luca: friends of Johnny Bopp. The plans were to smoke Jason Johnson the night before his wedding day. It would be payback for having him arrested on the day of his reception and for not accepting the bribe that he was offered.

Moe leaned back in his chair as he carefully studied the picture of the handsome young prosecutor who bore an uncanny resemblance to him. He commented to Vesurio saying that, "A guy who looks likes this could have the world at his feet. Yet he chooses to be a civil servant. What a waste."

Vesurio starred at the picture and commented, "Of course you think he's good looking because he looks like a younger version of you. Are you sure you don't know his Mama?" The two men broke into laughter.

Moe's cell rang it was his wife Reagan. "Moe, when are you coming home? I need you to take me to the Doctor's office at 3 p.m." Reagan's doctors' appointment was the last thing on Moe's mind. He had serious business to take care of but she needed him to go to with him. He smiled as he thought, "This is the price you pay for marrying someone as beautiful and as spoiled as Reagan Winters."

"Reagan I want you to listen up. I am going to be tied up for next couple of hours. Can't you get one of your friends to go with you to your appointment?"

Reagan sat on the side of the bed and began to whine into the phone. Whining was a character trait she possessed and one that he hated immensely.

"Moe I need you to go with me. The doctor is going to show the baby on the sonogram today. So you need to be there."

"Reagan I want you to listen up because I don't intend to repeat myself. I can't go!" As he hung up the phone he could still hear her whining and bitching.

This love thing with Reagan would have to be placed on the back burner. He had more important things to think about: like how to stay out of prison.

At the end of their meeting Vesurio invited Moe to go on the 'Baltimore's World famous Block' for a lap dance. Moe told him, "Man I don't need a lapdance. I can get a lap dance at home." He told Vesurio that more than a lapdance he needed a good head job. When he thought about it, he had not had any serious oral sex since Meagan.

"What I need is a bitch who can give serious head: someone with nice strong jaws. Now tell me do you know a bitch that can perform like that?"

Vesurio said, "I got two girls Sue Mae and Brit. Man these two are sensational! Sue Mae gives the best head on the planet and Brit can take it anyway you give it. Know what I mean?" Moe began to smile as his imagination began to kick in.

"Why don't you take a ride with me? I'll let you choose which one that you want. Laughingly he said, "Or maybe you'll want both?"

"Yeah man let me have both of them. One of them can give me head while the other tosses my salad."

"Whatever you want Moe." Changing his voice to sound like a young urban African American, he said, "You the man Moe!"

Moe said, "Make it clear to them that I don't want any conversation from them. I get enough conversation at home."

Vesurio laughed as he said, "Don't worry man. These two are fresh off the boat. They hardly speak or understand English."

The girls were better than the best. They gave him a sensational tongue bath and afterwards a nice warm hot-tub bath. As he was getting dressed he looked at the girls and said, "There is nothing like non-committal sex." The girls looked at each other and laughed. He doubted that the two Philippian girls knew what he was talking about.

After his encounter with Sue Mae and Britt, he felt as if he were on top of the world. He found himself whistling a love tune as he drove through downtown Baltimore to his mother's condo at the Harbor Place.

His mother, Fannie Blue-Light was now a fading beauty. She'd given up her escort service and was living large in her luxurious million-dollar waterfront home on the harbor.

Moe walked into his mother's condo, sat down at the piano and began to play Johnny Mathias' rendition of 'That's All'. Fannie joined him at the piano and began to sing: "I can only give you country lots in spring time and a hand to hold when leaves begin to fall...."

When they'd gone though a few of Fannie's favorites from her repertoire of show tunes, she asked her hunk of a son, "So what brings you to your poor old mother's house in the middle of the afternoon?"

"Mother I need you to look after my wife while I take care of my business."

"Moe what are you up to? You finally got yourself a decent woman and now you going to go and mess it up. I don't want any part of this foolishness!"

"Mama, why don't you hear me out? I got a few things that need to be taken care of and I need you to baby sit my spoiled wife."

"Moe are you fooling around on your wife? Listen to me son: I beg you, please don't be like your father."

It had been fifty years since his parents separated but his mother talked about it as if it were yesterday. "Mama it's not like that."

Fannie placing her hands over her heart as if in pain rendered a great imitation of Red Fox portraying a heart attack victim.

"Then pray tell me, what it is? And I hope to God that you aren't selling that stuff again because that would kill me! I mean if you had to go back to jail again. I would just lie down and die!"

Moe laughed out loud. He knew he could always get a laugh when he met up with his mother. Not only was Fannie pretty enough to have been a Hollywood starlet but she had all of the drama to go along with it.

Switching very quickly from melodramatic to low-key, "So Mr. Johnson, you think your mother is a joke?"

Moe putting on a serious face said, "No Mama. I love you. I just want you and Reagan to spend sometime together. You know what I mean, like get to know each other. Maybe the two of you could go to Vegas for a few days."

All Fannie needed was for Moe to say that he loved her. She opened her arms and embraced her son, telling him that she would be happy to take care of his wife for a few days.

28

The Irony of it All

The afternoon before the wedding, Jason's mother flew in from New York.

An English teacher by profession, Ms. Andrea Devereaux was perfectly polished and strikingly beautiful: the epitome of elegance and sophistication. She was elated to know that her son was marrying a beautiful and well-educated young woman. It had been decided that she would stay at her son's newly renovated Brownstone on Capitol Hill, while he and his bride honeymooned in Rome. She had not been to Washington, DC since her husband's death last October, so she was prepared to take full advantage of her week's stay in the District of Columbia. Her itinerary was full as she planned to shop, go sightseeing and maybe even look up a few friends. This would be the perfect opportunity to relax and reflect back over her life.

Jason's friends rented a suite at hotel in 'Pentagon City' for his Bachelor's party. They arrived at his house around 8:30 p.m., to pick him up.

His best-man Charles asked, "Hey Jason, are you ready for your last night as a free man? You do realize this is the last night that you can call yourself a single man?"

Jason smiled saying, "Yes, I'm ready. I just hope that you guys keep the entertainment simple."

He was tired and the last thing that he wanted was a bunch of half dressed women trying to seduce him. And then with a big smile he said, "Remember that I'm getting married at ten in the morning."

"Man why don't you loosen up? You don't have to be the federal prosecutor tonight. Man we've got girls coming that might make you change your mind."

Jason said, "Not even a proposal from Halle Berry could make me do that!"

Andrea showered and went to bed around 9:30 p.m. At 10:45 p.m., she heard what sounded like breaking glass on the first floor. She looked at the clock on the dresser and determined that it was too early for Jason to be returning home, and that it couldn't be Shanae because she talked to her less than a half hour ago. She wondered if someone were breaking into the house. And if someone were breaking in, why hadn't the alarm system gone off? She listened keenly as she heard footsteps on the stairs, coupled with what sounded like labored breathing. Slipping out of bed and down onto the floor, she carefully eased the phone off the hook and began to dial her son. In a whispered voice she told Jason that someone was in the house but before she could say another word she heard voices in her son's room.

Andrea whispering said, "Jason someone is in the house."

"Are you sure? Where are you in the house?"

"I'm in the guest room on the floor beside the bed."

Jason said, "Don't hang-up but don't talk anymore because they might hear you. Leave the phone open and try to make it into the closet without being heard. Look for the mirror at the back of the closet. On the other side of the mirror between my office and the bedroom is my gunroom. Push in on the right side of the mirror and stay behind the wall. You will be able to see and hear them but they won't see you. I'll be there shortly with the police."

Just as Andrea attempted to crawl to the closet, she heard a man say, "Did you check the other bedrooms?"

She felt her heart beating louder than usual as she crawled under the large mahogany bed.

The dark cherry wood floor was cold with tiny dust particles and she felt as if she were going to sneeze. A man with thick black rubber soled shoes walked around to examine both sides of the bed and then haphazardly looked into the closet. His breathing was labored as if he were in distress. The bed shook as he sat down on one side of it to rest. When a minute or two had passed, his accomplice walked into the room and told him to the check out the attic while he continued to search the rooms on the second floor.

When she was sure that they'd left the room, Andrea managed to crawl across the floor and into the closet. She glanced up to see her son's shirts hanging neatly according to color. There were yellow, blue and white shirts neatly hanging together. The smell of cedar and cologne infused her nostrils, as she wondered if she would live to see another day. Without standing up for fear of being discovered, she felt around the mirror until it opened then she carefully closed the door, and stood quietly behind it.

One of the men came back into the room, and then he left and came back with the other man. The thinner man asked, "Did you notice that this bed wasn't made?"

"No. I didn't pay attention."

"Did you even feel it, to see if it was warm?"

"No."

The thin man continued to interrogate his accomplice. "Did you even bother to check under the bed? Did it occur to you that the other beds were made?"

The heavy man walked to the other side of the bed but not before stumbling over one of Andrea's shoes. The thin man motioned to the heavier man that the phone was missing from the receiver.

At that point, the thin man motioned to the other man that someone might be hiding under the bed. The heavier man stood back, took aim and fired four shots into the mattress of the bed. With white down feathers flying everywhere, the two men pulled back the mattress, only to discover that no one was beneath it. The thinner man said "Someone is in this house and we need to get to them before they tip off the cops."

Both men went into the large walk-in closet and began rummaging through the prosecutor's neatly hung suits and shirts. It was the heavier man, who stopped to look in the mirror at his grotesque frame before commenting: "I promised my wife that I would loose a few pounds this year."

On the other side of the mirror Andrea was crouching in a corner hoping not to be discovered.

The heavier man asked, "Did you cut the phone line when you cut the alarm line?"

"No, I thought you did."

The thin man said, "Moe Johnson is paying big bucks for this job, so we can't afford to mess it up. Go downstairs and cut the telephone line."

When Andrea heard the name Moe Johnson, her heart skipped a beat. She thought, "How could Moe Johnson have a connection to this. It couldn't possibly be the same person that she'd been married to nearly thirty years ago. It had to be someone else because the Moe Johnson that she knew was probably still serving time in Federal prison on king pin charges.

The last time she saw Moe was the night he'd become so enraged about her going to one of his hang-outs for a drink, that he'd thrown her clothes out on the lawn. Attempting to gather her wits about her, she decided that her imagination was running wild because of the predicament that she was in.

Over on Massachusetts and 14th Streets, in the bridal suite, of a fabulous Capitol Hill hotel, Shanae's friends were giving her a banging bachelorette party. Around 11p.m. she asked if I would go with her to Jason's house to get her aunt's diamond necklace. "Erica, you know the saying is, that it's bad luck for the groom to see the bride the night before the wedding but I really need my diamond necklace." I am afraid that Jason's mom won't be able to find it and besides that, I don't want her rummaging through my personals: and more importantly I don't want her to see the toys that I purchased exclusively for the wedding night. So if you don't mind I'd like for you to go with me to Jason's house to pick it up. And just in case Jason is there, do you mind looking through my luggage to find it? I borrowed the necklace from my aunt. You know the cliché, something old, something new, something borrowed and something blue."

Of course I didn't mind going with her. I was tired of hearing all of the hell night stories from her sorority sisters. A ride to the other-side of town would be a welcomed change.
"No, I don't mind. Let's go."

Shanae and I arrived at Jason's at around 11:30 p.m. I got out of the car and walked up the picturesque tree-lined street to Jason's house. Just as I was about to ring the bell someone grabbed me from behind. Lifting me off the ground and into mid-air, he put his hand over my mouth. I kicked and fought as much as I could. The next thing I remembered was the man whispering very softly in my ear, telling me to be quiet and that he was an 'Alcohol, Firearms and Tobacco' agent.
The agent said, "I'm going to take my hand from your mouth but I want you to be very quiet. Can you be quiet? It is very important that you keep quiet."
I nodded yes. As he released me from his grip, I turned and looked into the eyes of my captor. It was Mark one of the groomsmen. He went on to say that, "Someone has broken into the house and Jason's mother is inside."
Thinking the worst, I asked, "Oh my God! Is she going to be okay?"
"We don't know. The phone line was open but now it appears that someone has cut the line.

I want you to go back to the car and wait."

Police officers and federal agents surrounded the house and eventually the police captain got on the mega-phone and ordered the assassins out of the house.

Inside the house the thin man said, "I am going to make a run for it". His counterpart, the heavier man said, "Go for it man. I'll cover you!"
"Are you sure?"
"I'm okay. Just get the hell out of here!"

The thin man went up the chimney and out on to the roof. He heard a helicopter in the distance as he crawled to the roof of an adjoining house. As he slithered down the drainpipe he spotted a screened patio door. He figured the alley below would be swarming with cops, so he took a chance by climbing onto the deck of the house. Methodically he lifted the screen from the slide, and slipped quietly into the house.

With his gun drawn he made his way down the narrow hall of the second floor. The house was dark and smelled of potpourri. A dim light shone from one of the bedrooms suggesting that someone was at home.
Entering the bedroom as inconspicuously as he had the house, he encountered a man and woman who were actively engaged in sex. The woman was on top of the man screaming to the top of her lungs and did not hear him as he crossed the threshold of the bedroom. Once inside the room he snatched the woman off the man, placing a gun to her head he ordered the man face down on the floor. He told them that the police would be doing a door-to-door search in about an hour and he did not want to be discovered.
"So if you want to live, do as I say. Is anyone else in the house?" Simultaneously, the man and woman both answered, "No."

Next he ordered the couple into the basement. Once the man was securely gagged and bound, the thin intruder ordered the woman back upstairs into the bedroom. He knew that it would not be long before the police would be doing a door-to-door search so he took his clothes off, put on a pair of the man's pajamas and climbed into bed with the wife. The wife seemed less terrified after her husband was in the basement. In fact it was she who opened her thighs without protest for the handsome stranger's entry. Little did she know that she would headline tomorrow's newspaper, "Congressman Tyler Branch and Wife Killed in Home Invasion?"

It was less than half an hour before the heavy guy decided to go DBP (death by police). He walked out of the house pointing his loaded gun at the police officers as he yelled, "Come on mother f_ckers! Let's see what you got!" Five officers pulled their guns and took him down. Minutes later he lay in the street in a pool of blood.

After the heavy man was shot and killed, the police infiltrated the house in search of other intruders. When the house was declared safe everyone went in side.

Andrea was visibly shaken as she told of the two men who shot into the bed, believing that she was under it. She refused medical attention, insisting that she had not been injured. The only thing that she asked for was a moment alone with her son.

"Jason I need to know something about Moe Johnson. "Why mother? Is it because you heard that he is the person trying to have me killed?"

Andrea nervously wringing her hands said "No it's because he maybe related to your father. Your father had a close relative whose name was Moe Johnson. Do you have a picture of him?" She wondered if her worst fear had finally come to fruition.

"And what if he is a relative? What good would it do for you to talk to this man?"

"Jason I am serious. I need to meet and talk with him."

Jason hearing the seriousness in his mother's voice said, "Even if he is a long lost cousin, his ass is still going down. Don't you realize that you could have been killed tonight? And if that had happened I would have taken the law into my own hands?"

"Jason Michael Johnson don't you ever threaten violence in my presence again. Whatever happened to your Christian training?

"Sorry Mom, I didn't mean to disrespect you but the thought of something like that happening to you makes me crazy."

"I'm okay. God spared my life."

Jason believing that his mother was not quite herself said, "Mom are you sure that you're okay? Why don't you let me take you to the hospital?"

"You can think that I'm crazy if you like but I have a feeling about this Moe Johnson. I feel that once he realizes that you're a relative he won't ever try to harm you again. The Johnson's are like that. They look out for their own."

After the attempt on Jason's life, some members of the bridal party, along with Shanae's parents decided to stay at Diamond's home for safekeeping.

It was Mark who drove us to Diamond's house. I sat in the front of his car and hung on to every word that he said. I liked the way that he talked. He told us that he'd received his Jurist Doctorate from Columbia University and he'd passed the Maryland Bar two weeks ago. I think I was intrigued with him for two reasons: the first was because he was an attorney and the second because he sounded much like my father. As we drove to Arlington, I fantasized about life with him. Maybe we could have the kind of life that my parents had.

Once he was sure that every one was safely inside, he left the house to sleep outside in his car.

I asked, "Why don't you come inside? I am sure that there is enough space for you. I could prepare one of the guest rooms for you." He said, that he'd promised Jason that he would stay with us to make sure that we were safe.

"How can I protect you, if I'm asleep? Why don't you go inside and get some rest."

I looked into his eyes and it was at this very moment that I knew that at last my knight in shinning armor had come.

29

"The truth shall set you free!"

A little more than a week after Jason returned from his honeymoon, Moe was picked up for questioning and prosecutors were trying desperately to revoke his bail. Andrea pleaded for a chance to meet with Moe. Jason finally gave in and arranged for his mother to meet with Moe. Andrea asked that she be allowed to meet him without recorders and without the presence of others. Jason thought his mother's request was strange but he granted it.

Andrea walked into the room and immediately recognized her estranged husband. He looked at her in disbelief and said, "Andrea, is it really you? What are you doing here?"

"Moe, we need to talk."

Regaining his composure he said, "About what? What do we have to talk about? You've got a lot of nerve walking in here after you abandoned me!"

"Moe, can't we try to be civil with each other?"

"The only thing that I want to know is what the hell are you doing here?"

Andrea said, "I guess I'd better get straight to the matter. A few weeks ago you tried to have the federal prosecutor killed at his house."

Moe looked in to Andrea's eyes and said, "Look woman I don't know what the hell you talking about. Why are you here-accusing me of this bullshit?"

"Moe I beg you to hear me out. It's not bullshit because I was at his house that night, and as a result I was nearly killed."

"I still don't understand how any of this concerns me."

"It concerns you because the man that you are trying to have killed is your son."

Moe screamed out, "What the hell are you talking about? Officer let me out of here! This woman is crazy!"

"Wait! Moe I need you to hear me out!"

Andrea stood and gestured to the officer, waving him away from the door. "Moe, you know that I'm not a liar."

Moe was suspicious of his ex-wife's presence and even more of the conversation. "Andrea I don't know anything about you or who you've become. I haven't seen you since you left me nearly thirty years ago. Woman you can't imagine how much you hurt me!" The anger that he'd been holding back for so many years suddenly resurfaced and he felt like backhanding her. She sensed his anger and knew that she had to gain control of the situation.

She said, "What about me? I was also hurt! Do you remember that it was you who threw me out! On that last night, I came home happy and excited. I was going to tell you about the baby when I found all of my belongings on the lawn. And when I thought about it, I decided I didn't want to raise a child around violence and drugs. Thank God that I left. Our son is a decent law-abiding citizen: a federal prosecutor!"

Moe gathering his wits about him thought about everything that just transpired. Although, what she said made sense but to believe what she was saying, meant defying all logic and reasoning. But he remembered that Andrea was an honest and a good woman, and for what reason would she have to lie about her son.

Everyone involved had commented on how much the prosecutor looked like him but he'd passed it off as coincidence. What a predicament he'd found himself in. The realization that he'd almost killed his son, made him nauseous and he threw up.

"Moe are you okay? Officer, can you please get him something to drink?"

The officer responded very sarcastically, "What should I get him? Does he want wine or beer?"

"Please sir, I think he's sick!"

Moe began to speak out saying, "All of the years that I spent in prison wishing that I'd had a child, someone who would love me unconditionally and all the time I had a son." He covered his face with his hands and when he removed his hands his eyes were filled with tears.

Somehow he managed to say, "What did you tell him about his father? I mean about me?"

"I told him that you died in a car accident. He believed me without question and because he never knew you he accepted my husband as his father. After all, Malcolm was the only father that he'd ever known."

Moe was perplexed and full of anxiety as he told her, "I understand. You did what you thought was best for him. What about your husband? Does he know who I am?"

"I told him the same thing that I told Jason. You see Malcolm was a good man, a minister, and he loved Jason as if he were his son. When he died last year Jason took it real hard. But you know I still find it strange that Jason never allowed Malcolm to adopt him. His name is Jason Michael Johnson."

"You gave him my middle name." Moe smiled because he felt a sense of pride knowing that his son had been named after him.

Andrea said, "When I heard you went to prison for life, I knew that I'd done the right thing by not telling him the truth but now I'm not so sure because you are trying to kill him!"

The very thought of him trying to kill his own flesh and blood suddenly made him crazed, and he screamed out in anguish saying, "Don't say that! Woman, don't you ever say that again!"

Andrea broke down sobbing uncontrollably.

Moe rose up from his chair, embracing her he said, "This changes everything. I'm going to find a way to make things right between us but first I need to get out of here. I will probably be released in about an hour because they don't have anything to hold me on. I want you to meet me at Quincy's restaurant in Union Station at two this afternoon. Can you meet me?"

"Yes, I'll be there. I would do anything to protect my son. Or should I say our son."

Moe's voice was stern as he said, "I don't want Jason to know that you are meeting me. Can I trust you Andrea?"

Andrea had begun daydreaming: floating back in time, to a time when she loved Moe more than anything in the world. He had been the best looking, the brightest, and the most athletic guy on Morgan's campus. And at fifty-two he was just as good-looking and sexy as he was twenty-eight years ago. She wondered if he could still hit it and make her scream: or if his oral prowess were as good as back in the day. She suddenly realized that her desire for him was as great as it was before she left him. She heard him talking to her but she'd found herself distracted and dreaming about a futuristic romantic escapade with him.

"Andrea, are you listening to me?"

She was startled by the interruption of her fantasy. "Yes Moe, I heard you. You want me to meet you at Quincy's in Union Station at two."

"Timing is everything. I need you to be on time. Can I trust you to do that for me?"

Unbeknown to her she'd slipped back into the role of being Moe's submissive wife.

Andrea very passively answered, "You know that you can trust me."

It was late in the afternoon when Andrea and Moe met. Andrea was hoping for a late lunch with cocktails and later some afternoon delight, but Moe had other plans. She was the first to arrive at Quincy's. She was dressed very smartly in a yellow and white corset dress that accentuated her cheerleader figure. She asked for a table in the rear for privacy. She wanted this gorgeous man all to herself.

Moe arrived at exactly five minutes after two. Walking into the restaurant he commanded an audience. He was meticulous from collar to cuff in his grey and white pinstriped shirt and black pants. Several women groups having tea, or meetings of varied social functions, took notice when he walked in. Some of the women openly flirted with him, as he made his way to the back of the restaurant where Andrea sat waiting for her man.

It was apparent that time had been very kind to Andrea for she radiated extraordinary beauty and for a second, Moe also appeared to be caught up in the moment.

The ambiance was right, and Andrea took the opportunity to lean across the table and kiss Moe on his lips. He surprised himself when he kissed her back with the same passion that she exuded.

After regaining his composure, he wiped her lipstick from his lips and said, "Don't do this Andrea".

"Do what? What Am I doing?"

Drea listen up, "I don't have time for this. I didn't come here for this."

Andrea very coyly asked, "Whatever do you mean?"

Moe not wanting to waste time took command of the situation and quickly made his point.

He said, "I'm going to give you the key to one of my safe deposit boxes."

Andrea was surprised. "Why? What 's in your safe deposit box?"

"There is jewelry totaling about half a million and another four hundred 'G's' in cash. I want you to have it."

"But why are you giving it to me?"

"Just consider it the child support that you never collected."

"Moe, I can't accept the money or the jewelry. It wouldn't be right."

"Okay, you don't have to accept it but I want you to make a will and leave the money to my son." You can do whatever you like with the jewelry."

"What about you? Won't you need the money for your defense?"

Moe hesitated saying, "No, I'm okay. Anyway I'm going away for awhile."

"Where are you going?"

"I can't tell you that but I promise to keep in touch with you."

With lust in her heart and desperation in her voice Andrea said, "If you leave now, I know that I'll never see you again. And I really want to see you again."

Without a doubt Andrea had fallen once again for Moe Johnson. He couldn't believe that she still had a thing for him. He wished that he'd had the time to make love to her but he had a train, and then a plane to catch. His plan was to be in San Juan, by tomorrow morning. He'd been there two years ago and he had good friends who lived there. He knew he could depend on his friends to keep him safe from the authorities and that his international looks would make it easy for him to blend in with the masses.

Andrea would never realize that Moe was extending her more of a courtesy than he had to his wife. He had no intention of dealing with Reagan's spoiled self-centered ass. For sure he would make certain that she and the baby would be well provided for but that would be the extent of it. She'd become a big pain in his ass!

"Andrea, I promise that you will hear from me as soon as I get settled".

"Some how I don't believe you."

"Believe me because you are going to be my contact person in the states because I know that you'd be the last person that the feds would expect that I'd be in contact with."

"Where will you go? How will I contact you?"

"You won't be able to contact me. I'll have to contact you. Also, I want you to get in contact with Fannie. Keep the line of communication open with her. I want her to meet her grandson before she dies. I know that she would be so proud to know how he turned out."

Andrea very softly said, "Maybe I will. Maybe I will."

Andrea got up from her chair and sat directly beside Moe. Their eyes did the lovers dance before she placed her lips on his and whispered, "Moe take me with you." Moe put his arm around her and pulled her close to him and gave her the most gentle and sweetest kiss she'd ever known.

Holding her in his arms, he contemplated the thought of how different his life might have been if he'd had a wife and son to love and care for. He wondered if he might have given up life in the fast lane. Maybe he would have tried out for the Olympic track team, or even become a physical education teacher. Hell, his high school music teacher once said that he had the makings of a concert pianist. It hurt to know that with all of his talent, he was just another convict on the run.

Leaning back in his chair he said, "Drea, I am on the run and I need to disappear for a while. Besides what kind of life would it be for you constantly moving with no real direction? What would you tell our son? What you're asking is impossible. The best I can offer is a phone call now and then, or at least until I can work things out."

Moe reached under the table and handed Andrea a small black leather case. "I want you to take this. It contains the keys to one of my safe deposit boxes. You will also find some of my personal papers and how to get in touch with my mother.

He got up from the table, leaned over and kissed his ex-wife on the forehead. Then he whispered in her ear, "I never stopped loving you Drea." Cupping her face with his hands he said, "In fact now that I think about it, you are the only woman that I ever loved. I need you to promise me that no matter what ever else that you hear you will believe that! Oh yeah, there's one more thing that I need you to do", his voice suddenly breaking with emotion. "If you decide to tell Jason that I'm his father. Tell him that I didn't know. And tell him that I love him and if he ever needs me … I mean for anything. What the hell am I talking about? Why would he need me? In his eyes I am just another convict."

Andrea feeling her ex-husband's pain said, "Moe don't say that. He will change his mind once he knows who you are, just as you have changed your feelings for him."

Moe having made his peace with his former wife beckoned the waiter and paid the check. As he walked away he turned back to say, "I'll call you soon." With tears streaming from her face Andrea called out unashamedly across the restaurant, "Moe don't leave me. Please don't leave me!"

Jason met his mother at the door, when she returned home. She fell into his arms and began to cry. When she was able to regain her composure, she said, "Jason, there is something that I have to tell you.

"It's okay Mom. I already know. I know he's my father."

"But how could you know?"

"It didn't take a rocket scientist to figure it out, especially after you kept insisting that he might be a relative. Aside from the fact that we have the same middle and last name: it was the way that you insisted on talking with him and assuring me that he would never hurt me if he knew that I was a relative. His profile indicates that the only persons that he might not harm would be his mother and his child."

"Now that you know who he is are you still going to prosecute him because he honest to God didn't know about you? You should have seen how upset he was when he found out that he was your father. He told me to tell you that he didn't know about you and that he loves you."

"Mom, why don't you listen to yourself? How could he love me when he doesn't even know me? He tried to have me killed and in the process he almost killed you! Anyhow he's gone now, and I hope that it's for good."

"Please don't talk like that. Give him a chance."

"Give him a chance to do what? I gave him a chance for a new life, when I allowed him to board the plane for Puerto Rico this afternoon."

"Listen to me! He's your father!"

"He's not my father! My father died last year. Malcolm Devereaux was my father."

"Moses Michael Johnson is your biological father."

"He was the sperm donor!"

"Don't talk like that! I told you that he didn't know about you."

"It's a good thing that he didn't know about me because I could have been a drug-dealer like him! Think about it mother: what if I'd turned out to be a drug-dealer? Now how would you feel about that? Would we be having this conversation if I were a drug dealer?"

"Don't be disrespectful! I will not tolerate disrespect!"

"Okay, I'm sorry. I just want you to look at things realistically. See the man for what he is."

"And how did you know that he was leaving the country?"

"It's my job to know everything."

"He wants you to meet his mother, your grandmother."

"I need some time to think about that."

"You're angry with, me aren't you? Son please don't be angry with me!"

Jason put his arm around his mother and said "Angry? Why should I be angry with you? Like always you did what you thought was best for me, and I could never be angry about that."

30

Dear Diary, No more Drama!

Things were finally beginning to settle down and most of the drama in my life had subsided. My best friend Kennedy was married to the love of her life, and attending Parsons. Last weekend when I visited with her in New York, we saw 'The Color Purple'. It was my first Broadway show. After the show Kennedy introduced me to one of the actors and we had a late night dinner in So-ho. I love the fast pace of New York. It is the most exciting place that I've ever been and the shopping is best. But most importantly, I can't believe that my best friend is really one hundred percent in-love and dedicated to her husband.

Madison joined the Peace Corps and is stationed in Kenya. This was a good move for her because she was not ready for college.

Diamond is no longer juggling two relationships because she and Burton have finally set a date. As for Grandpa Clayton, he is seriously dating a Ms. Minnie Moto, someone he met at the 'National Native American POW Wow'.

Sidney just returned from a visit to England and he was proud to report that Meagan was engaged to an officer in the military, and she'd begun classes at Oxford University.

Poor Reagan had a slight breakdown after the miscarriage of her baby and she is recuperating at Fannie's home in Baltimore.

Jason and Shanae are expecting a little girl and Andrea is planning a rendez-vous with Moe in Puerto Rico.

31

Wishing on a Star

Crickets and birds chirped, while deer danced playfully on the back lawn.

Tonight was one of those mystical summer evenings, when nature plays tricks with your emotions.

In the background I heard Diamond singing the lyrics of Natalie Cole's version of 'That Sunday that Summer'. Through the palladium windows, I watched as she sliced and diced carrots, tomatoes and leeks. Just watching this ritual gave me an unbelievable surge of contentment because at last my grandmother was doing the grandmother thing, preparing home cooked meals.

As I lay on the deck of my grandmother's Arlington home, there appeared to be a million stars in the sky tonight, but I was wishing on only one: the one that would bring Mark and I together. Tomorrow would be my first official date with Mark. Although, I still can't figure out why he still wanted to see me, especially after overhearing the phone conversation that he'd had with Diamond earlier in the afternoon.

"My granddaughter is only eighteen years old and you are twenty-four years old. And by the way did you know that she is a virgin? Or do you like robbing young women of their virtue?"

When Mark was able to get a word in he said, "With all due respect Mrs. Redfern, your granddaughter is of legal age and she seems capable of making her own decisions."

It did not matter to Diamond that this man was a federal agent because she was ready to take him on.

"If you do anything to hurt her, it will become personal! Do we understand each other?"

Diamond continued to question him, asking him about his intentions as far as I was concerned.

Mark in a mad chill said, "We are going to cruise down to St. Michael's and then to Annapolis. My godparents will also be on board. Is that okay with you? By the way, would you like to join us?"

Very sarcastically she replied, "Don't tempt me!"

Mark picked me up at noon. I wore a red, white and blue nautical pants set and Diamond's blue and white Captain's hat. I must have checked my image in the mirror a dozen times before he arrived. Why was I so nervous? I guess because he was older and more sophisticated. Everything had to be right!

I walked up on deck and sat in the captain's chair pretending to be the master of all I surveyed. A few minutes later he came from behind and began to gently massage my shoulders. This was an awkward moment for me because what if he was being brotherly or what if he wanted a kiss. And what kind of a kiss was he looking for? I wished that I'd had some insight into what he really wanted from me.

Lunch was the most awkward time of all. We ate with three other couples, all recent law school graduates. One of the girls Robin finished law school with Mark. It was when she asked me about the new birth control on the market that I got a reality check.

She said, "I am sick of the pill and the shot makes me physically sick. Erica, what are you using?"

My face was blank.

I didn't know how to respond, so I excused myself and made a mad dash for the bathroom. Robin followed behind me asking, "Are you okay? Is it something that you ate?"

From behind the closed door, I said, "I'll be fine."

Damn why doesn't she leave me alone! I wished that she would go away but she just stood there making unnecessary conversation.

"By the way, did you know that Mark and I dated during law school?"

"No, I hadn't heard."

Laughing she said, "No, of course you haven't. You were probably in middle school or playing house with your little friends."

As far as I was concerned, she had crossed the line. Using my no nonsense voice I said, "So what is your point?"

"I'm not trying to make a point. I just thought you might like to know."

"Do I have a choice?"

"We were an item for about three years. When I think about it, I should have married him."

I was infuriated by her remarks, "So why are you telling me this."

"No reason. I just thought you might want to know a few things about your man."

"Like what?"

"Like the fact that he likes a lot of sex but I suppose you already know that."

I felt inadequate, sort of like I'd come unprepared for a final exam. "If you don't mind, I'd like to be alone. In fact I think I may throw-up!"

"Okay girl, I'm outta here."

Suddenly I realized that being with Mark was entirely too much work. I was just too young for this kind of a relationship. If all things were equal I wouldn't have to work so hard at trying to be mature. With guys my age everything had a natural flow but with Mark I felt inadequate: sort of like I was in the wrong place. This wasn't fun. It was too hard trying to figure out what to say and what to do to keep a twenty-four year old interested.

When he took me home, I surprised myself when I told him, "It was a lovely after noon but this isn't working for me and I won't be seeing you again."

"What do you mean? Did I do or say something that you didn't like? What's wrong?"

"No you were a perfect gentleman. In fact you're the best!"

"Then what's the problem? Why don't you want to see me again?"

All of a sudden he looked really old to me. His demeanor, his conservative style no longer worked for me and I made the decision to be brutally frank.

"It's because you're too old to be my first!"

"Erica, we have a six year age difference between us. How important is six years, if two people are attracted to each other?

"I guess it's like my grandmother said, I need to live a little before I get serious with anyone and besides Robin told me quite a lot about the two of you."

"What exactly did she say?"

"More than I needed to know."

"Did she tell you that I caught her in my Jacuzzi making love to my friend?"

"No, she left that part out."

"She also should have told you that she is still calling me and asking me to take her back?"

"No, she forgot that part."

"If you want to know anything about me she's not the one to ask! Robin is a jealous viper!"

"To be honest with you, it's not only the things that Robin told me. It's the fact that you've already done everything that I need to do."

"What exactly is that?"

"For one thing, I need to finish college, and get my career going. I will be starting college in two weeks and I'll need to concentrate on my schoolwork. So you see I won't have time for a serious relationship."

"Erica, don't do this!"

"I have to."

"Give us a chance!"

"I'm sorry." I partially opened the car door and attempted to exit when Mark grabbed me by my arm. I could tell that he was mad but he was smart enough to understand that no meant no.

"Can I at least call you?"

"I suppose there is nothing wrong with talking on the phone."

After dinner I told Diamond of my decision not to see Mark again, she smiled and told me how much I'd matured.

Looking back over my life this past year, there had been a conglomeration of events that changed my life forever. The most catastrophic was the loss of my parents but the one truly sublime thing that I would cherish and hold dear for the rest of my life: my relationship with my grandmother.

Diamond is my best friend.

978-0-595-47030-3
0-595-47030-0

Printed in the United States
138123LV00002B/2/P